NORTH EAST of SCOTLAND LIBRARY SERVICE
14 Crown Terrace, Aberdeen

'Hard Shining Corn' and the stories which follow it splendidly capture a way of life that has disappeared. The deprivation, the vicious exploitation and the contrasting fullness of life of "cottar folk" in north-east Scotland are portrayed, movingly and humourously, and with the kind of emotion that comes only from a writer with an immediate and urgent experience of his subject. David Toulmin has tempered his Doric for this, his first book, and there should be nothing to frighten off an adventurous reader from south of the border.

David Toulmin is the pen name of John Reid, who now lives in retirement in Aberdeen after over 40 years as a farm servant. His formal education ended on his fourteenth birthday at a rural Aberdeenshire school and he began work the following day as a 'fee'd loon' for £6.50 per half year.

He first wrote a short story in 1947 and since then has produced a social panorama of Buchan and the Mearns, earlier this century, that would do credit to one born to the pen and not the ploughshare. A number of his stories have been broadcast by the BBC.

HARD SHINING CORN

David Toulmin

IMPULSE BOOKS

Aberdeen

First published 1972 by
Impulse Publications Ltd.,
28 Guild Street,
Aberdeen.

ISBN A1605

To Margaret Jane.

AbT2
––––
9

960336

Typeset by Martin Dawson
and printed by The Langstane Press, Aberdeen.

CONTENTS

Introduction by John R. Allan

INTRODUCTION

by John R. Allan

It is a real pleasure to introduce the world of David Toulmin. Introduce is not quite the right word, for most of the stories and sketches have already appeared in newspapers and magazines or been broadcast on Radio. It is a good thing they have now been gathered together, thus giving a wider picture of a way of life.

It is the life of the men and women on the farms of Aberdeenshire in particular, but general to all the East of Scotland. It is a life I am very familiar with, sometimes to my regret, and I can say that David Toulmin has written about it with truth and spirit. It is not exactly of today but I guess of forty odd years ago, so the stories are of time remembered, and a gie thrawn time at that.

Farm work was ill paid and farmers were not always the kindliest of employers. There were many workers who thought of farmers as their natural enemies, in spite of the good ones who were nearly as kind to men as to cattle. David Toulmin catches this feeling again and again as he describes the working conditions in field and byre and midden and the living conditions in the cottar houses and chaumers that were sometimes nearly middens themselves. But many of the folk who lived so had wit and humour, and that has been caught very well too, though the language is politer than much I remember from the time I was a loon in the days before the Permissive Society, when in fact anything not permitted was both said and done.

There are three chapters I like particularly. The first is about a young couple's day at Aikey Fair, true and simple and charming. The second is the portrait of Rab of the Barnyards. He was the grieve who could get a power of work out of any squad, enough to satisfy the most demanding farmer, and at the same time made it up to the squad by stealing and sharing with them the farmer's milk and corn and coal. In the thirties there were quite a few characters like that, men of vast resources who became local legends. The third story I like is called "I Wadna Be A Loon Again," and is about a hard apprenticeship. Anybody that was a farm loon forty years ago will say "Aye" to that.

I end as I began by saying that the book is a pleasure and I hope it gets the good hairst of success it deserves.

John R. Allan, Little Ardo, Methlick.
July 26, 1971.

HARD SHINING CORN.

Shinbrae was a fine hill farm, well set up on the brae above its neighbours. The farmhouse squared its shoulders to the four winds with a sullen dignity, and the steading stood out boldly behind it in brazen austerity. Looking from the road Shinbrae had a dour "wha daur meddle wi' me?" aspect which intimidated the Seedsman's agent and prospective employee alike. It brought them wheedling to the back kitchie door with a respect which Shinnie played up well when it came to a chinwag.

Shinnie's black nowt could be seen for miles, the admiration and the envy of the countryside, fat and sleek as moles, and the sheep crawled like lice on the wide green slopes of Wild White clover. Wild White wasna lang in the go, and it fair took a hold on the hard, sun-drenched knowes at Shinbrae. Shinnies sometimes ploughed down a sole of tassled clover that mony a crofter lad would have been glad tae graze on. Auld Snorlie frae Swineden had tae tether his horse at the roadside, and sometimes herd a coo or twa, on "the lang acre" as he called it, 'cause there was nae grass in his parks, naething but steens and thistles, and there was only a stone dyke atween him and Shinnies. But Shinnies held on the herrin' guts and bone meal no end, and even dulce from the seaside, and though it rotted a corn crap or twa it fair put heart in the grun.

There was an avenue of beech and plane trees leading to the main road and the cottar houses at the entrance. Half down the hill, in the middle of a park was a windmill, 'cause there was no

drinking water on the place, and it had to be pumped up to a
cistern by the kitchen door, which also supplied the cottars.
Surface water that came down the hill was caught in the
milldam, closè by the steading and the stackyard. And man,
Shinnie's stackyard was worth looking at — every ruck shaved
with a scythe and thatched with green rushes from the peat-
bog, and diced over in diamond squares of golden straw-rapes,
each rick as trim as a giant beeruskie, with a wee pirn on top
like an ornament.

Shinnies thrashed out well, hard shining corn that had a fine
reeshle aboot it, grown on those hard flinty braes where you
couldn't put a foot down without standing on a pebble. To a
stranger Shinbrae was just a litter of stones and silly folk said
they should all be gathered off. But Shinnie's predecessors had
all been as wise as Solomon and left the flintstones alone. Man
they fair kept the moisture in a dry summer and filtered it
through in a wet season. Almost every sprouted grain had to
push a stone aside before it saw the light, and then the sun was
caught on the brae and polished it on the stalk. No wonder that
Shinnie put his thumbs in the armholes of his waistcoat on
threshing days, when he showed his gold dust to the neighbours.

But if a man was to be judged by the appearance of his farm
buildings maybe Shinnie wasn't all that bad. "Damned bigsy
thing" folk said, a gentleman farmer his wye o't, always
respectably dressed in a suit of brownish grey coarse tweed, a
watchchain across his waistcoat, collar and tie and jaunty cap.
His shoes were the squeaky type, brown like peasemeal, and
always betrayed his silent, thief-like approach. His moustache
was always neatly trimmed and the way he curled his lip over
his scented pipe you could say there was a quirk in the man
somewhere. His eyes were blue and clear but beady as a fox,
and when he looked at you you felt he was wondering how
he could wheedle a copper out of you more than he was
bargained for.

Furthermore Shinnie had the first motor car in the district,
a big Chevrolet with a canvas hood that fair gaed tearin' by
the ither lads still in their gigs. It stood mostly at the front
door as a sort of ornament to impress folks that came in by.

10

Almost every winter evening Shinnie went to the byre, handling his fat stots to see if they were ready for the butcher. You could always tell if Shinnie was about in the dark because you could feel the scented smell of his tobacco. It sort of charmed the air and though you didn't see the man you sort of liked him in spite of yourself.

But Shinnie was good enough to his cottars and they stayed on with him from year to year if there was nothing better in the market. Shinnie just let them know from the start that he would stand no nonsense and usually he had little bother with his workers. But he had been watchin' yon foreman chiel 'cause folk said he was a bit tarry fingered and couldn't let go of anything he got hold of in the dark. And yon second-horseman's wife was a bit of a claik and had abody's character in the district, and folk she didna like she gaed oot and cried at them on the road. Faith aye, Shinnie was sometimes black affronted at the limmer but put up wi' her 'cause her man was sic a sober, hard-workin' stock.

And Shinnie ay had a kind work for yon Charlie Stoddart, him that sortet Shinnie's nowt and pulled his neeps though the rain was running down his chin. Folk said Charlie was a bittie simple but he tore on at his work and pleased Shinnie fine whatever they said. And there was yon scrat o' a loon o' Charlie's that threw stones on the slates and broke the skylichts and tore doon the dykes lookin' for rabbits. He would be a problem to Charlie yon loon yet, him that wore his father's breeks and kissed the quines on the sly. A big loon like that fleein' aboot wi' a gird or his father's bicycle when he should be helpin' the old man in the byre.

But for all that Shinnie never said much to Charlie's loon, just curled his forefinger over the stem of his pipe and spat out a few hints ahin Charlie's back. "Dinna throw steens on the slates loon, ye could brak' the skylichts", or "that dyke ye knocket doon lookin' for rabbits — d'ye hear? Ye'll big it up again!" And the loon would behave himself for a fortnight, never a stain in his life, and he would square up beside Shinnie in the byre like he had a share in the place, and Shinnie would wait or Charlie's back was turned and then spit out at the

11

loon: "Dinna big stibble ruckies in yon park min, ye'll ruin my new grass!" Dash it, there was no pleasin' the man, so the loon would wipe his slate real clean and live like a quine for weeks on end, never striking a match about the place, nor even taking a drag at the old man's pipe, and then in the byre when the lanterns were lit he'd stand real close to Shinnie, his face shining with innocence and Shinnie would blame him for taking the prop out of a leaning haystack. "Can't ye let things alane, man?"

When Charlie's loon thrashed the foreman's loon coming home from school he never let on at home. But by byre time Shinnie had wind of it. "Ye thrashed the foreman's loon the day man!" "Oh ay," says the loon, "but he deserved it, even his ain brither said so, and he saw us fechtin'. He's been giein' me the coordie lick for a lang time, and stickin' his nieve in my face every day or I could stand it nae langer, so I let flist at him when he least expected it. He was a bloody mess by the time I finished wi' him but his brither never interfered. Maybe it'll teach 'im a lesson."

Shinnie looked at Charlie's loon almost in sympathy, then he removed his pipe and spat in the urine channel. "Ay laddie, but he's a bit younger than you, and so is his brother, and likely their father will have his ain back on you for that yet. He's a spiteful mannie the foreman once his birse is up."

Now Charlie's loon kept a pair of tame rabbits, a white Jack Rabbit and his blue-coated wife. A pair of cannibals they were and between them they had eaten seven litters of young. When the young were littered the loon put the Jack Rabbit in quarantine, but it made no difference, the mother merely dined more sumptuously and one by one the young disappeared. And it wasn't that he neglected them for the nickum took great pride in his rabbits. Almost any day you could see the crater miles from home with his little hand-cart searching for some delicacy for the hutch, a milky thistle, dandelions, big red clovers that waved in the wind like pom-poms.

Shinnie came to hear of the laddie's rabbits and in the byre one evening at supperin' time he said: "Ay lad, and how are

12

the rabbits doin'?"

"Oh fine", said the loon, "except that they've eaten their young again".

"Oh man, that's a peety noo".

There was a brief pause in which you could hear the nowt rattling their neck chains. Shinnie took his pipe from his mouth and spat on the greep.

"But lad", says he, pipe in hand, "what dae ye feed yer rabbits on?"

'Neeps", says Charlie's loon, seeing it was winter and no fresh grass in the fields.

"Neeps man!" said Shinnie, in a tone and expression of accusation.

"Ay neeps!" the loon repeated, all innocence, preparing himself for some advice on a change of diet for the carnivorous rabbits.

"And whaur dae ye get the neeps lad?" Pipe back in mouth, his hands in his trouser pockets Shinnie leaned back on his heels awaiting a confession.

The loon was completely unaware of the trap Shinnie had sprung for him. "Oh, oot o' your park", he stumbled.

Shinnie took a squint at old Charlie at the other end of the byre. He put his forefinger over his pipe stem and removed it from his set teeth. His eyes glittered down on the loon and his moustache bristled into single hairs. "Weel", he snarled, his lips curling into speech, "that wunna dee, ye understand? Lat there be nae mair o't, d'ye hear? Nae mair stealin' neeps. I canna be expectet tae grou neeps tae feed your rabbits on!"

Shinnie turned his back on the loon and went to feel his stots, fondling their flanks where the beef rippled under his fingers like a new wallet, and he put his arm under the warm hoch to feel the firm scrotum on each animal, an indication of their prime condition. He scratched the roots of their itching tails till they forgot their food and twisted their mouths in ecstasy.

The loon watched Shinnie with a lump in his throat and choked back the tears. He had thought himself further in with Shinnie than this and disappointment rankled him sorely.

13

And the beasts never kicked Shinnie, his touch was gentle and smooth as velvet, and they stopped chewing the cud and looked round at him with great liquid eyes, beseeching and full of trust, while he lured them to their deaths with doting care and loving kindness.

But Shinnie never kept heifers; they were restless and noisy before their menstruations and disturbed the whole byre. Nothing like quietness and peace to get a beast fat, and though some said that quaiks or heifers got fat sooner and gave quicker returns Shinnie still preferred a good stot with more weight in the carcass at the kill out.

But the loon wasn't long out of favour with Shinnie, for Charlie his father took the 'flu and went off work. And daggit if Shinnie didn't have the impudence to go and rap on Charlie's door and ask his wife if he could have the loon to help in the byre with Charlie's nowt. The beasts would miss the smell of old Charlie and the tone of his voice. They were fickle with strangers and would lose condition. It was hard work and Shinnie didn't like hard work, but he would get Charlie's loon to help and he would do the job himself.

For nearly six months now the beasts had been chained, coming almost fat from the pastures to hay and swede turnips, bruised corn and oilcake, and it wouldn't do to let them lag and lose money now. Very soon now the chains would be loosed from their necks and the beasts would break in a panic from the stalls, prancing blindly through the byre like mad demons in their new liberty. But Shinnie would give them twenty-minutes on the soft sharn midden where they would sink to their bellies and lose their high spirits before going on the road to the railway station. A few hours of precious freedom and the poor devils would have to pay for Shinnie's kindness under the butcher's hatchet.

Charlie's loon ran three miles to school on a dry piece and when he got back he bolted his dinner and went to help Shinnie in the byre.

Shinnie lit the lanterns and put the match to his pipe. He had his jacket off and his sleeves rolled up and the loon had never seen him like this before.

14

"Man", says he, "yer father's a grand worker but he's affa sair on the broom. He's hard on the besom and sair on himsell. He kills 'imsell, the breet!"

The loon looked up at Shinnie but didn't say anything. He knew he could never sweep the byre to please his father and he knew the old man raxed his guts with the old turnip slicer. Shinnie wasn't the man to thank him for it but at least he noticed it.

"Ay man", Shinnie continued, "and how are the rabbits doin'?"

"Oh they're starved tae death", said the loon, telling a lie to shun the devil.

"And what dae ye feed them on nooadays when ye dinna get a neep tae gie them?"

"Tea-leaves and meal", said the loon, wondering what Shinnie would say next.

"Och laddie", says Shinnie, "but ye can tak' a neep; ye canna hunger the craters!"

On the Sunday morning, when the loon went to feed his rabbits they were both dead with their throats cut. The murderer hadn't pommelled them in the usual bloodless way but had slit their throats hatefully and thrown them back in the hutch.

After breakfast Charlie's loon got a spade out of the toolshed and went to bury his rabbits in the backyard. And who should appear but the local bobby, followed by Shinnie and the foreman from next door. They went straight to the foreman's coalshed where they took a sackful of something from the interior. The foreman was made to shoulder it on his back, and then he walked in front of Shinnie and the bobby up the beech avenue to the farm.

What could it mean? The constable about the place on a Sunday morning brought all the cottars to their doors and windows. And what could the foreman have to do with it? Charlie's loon dropped his spade and ran inside to tell his old man. Maybe he could tell the bobby about his rabbits. Maybe he could find out who killed them.

Charlie Stoddart was still in his box-bed in the kitchen. But he wouldn't hear of his loon telling the bobby about his rabbits. "Na na", says he, "better haud yer tongue aboot it; we dinna want tae get enveigled wi' the bobby".

The foreman's wife watched her husband from the cottage door, the bairns around her, like Christian's wife in "The Pilgrim's Progress", when Christian set out with his bundle of sin upon his back.

The trio marched up the avenue, the foreman with his sack, the policeman and Shinnie, past the farmhouse, where the mistress and the kitchiedeem were glowerin' from the window, the single lads keekin' from the chaumer, right up the close to the loft door at the top of the stone steps.

Up in the lift the foreman dropped his sack. "Put it there!" said the bobby, indicating the weighing machine. The sack weighed eighty pounds. Shinnie untied the string and lifted a handful of his "Golden Rain" seed corn and ran it through his fingers.

Now Shinnie had been real cunning to catch the foreman. He looked like a lad who wouldn't have stolen a worm from a hen, yet here he was thievin' Shinnie's corn to feed his poultry. Shinnie had seen him going to the loft now and then, usually about dinner time, but thought maybe it was a pucklie bruised corn for his horse the lad was after. But Shinnie got suspicious and one day he followed the foreman on the sly. So the lad gaed right through the stable with the sack, out at the back door and into the millhouse, where he hid it in the shadows.

The old wheelhouse was an excellent place for concealment, damp and secretive, and the fall of the water under the wheel drowned every sound. Even when the wheel was stationary nobody ventured much into the wheelhouse; it was slippery and dangerous at all times, and after dark a veritable death-trap. It was at the back of the steading, away from the farmhouse, where even the collie dog couldn't hear anything.

Shinnie watched the foreman but stayed out of sight and never opened his trap. At yokin' time he newsed up the foreman as if he was his most trusted disciple. "Weel weel Wullie, juist haud back tae the ploo again."

But as soon as the horsemen had pulled out of the stable with their pairs Shinnie gaed roon the back and had a look in

16

the wheelhouse. He found the sack of oats in a bucket of the water-wheel, to be lifted after dark, when the foreman came back to supper his horse.

Shinnie 'phoned the bobby to come up to Shinbrae after dark and the two of them hid in the wheelhouse and waited for the thief. There wasn't a whiff from Shinnie's pipe, not a squeak from his shoes, and the foreman came and lifted his sack, unaware of the two pairs of eyes and ears lurking in the darkness. But they never molested him, just followed him right home to his coalshed with the sack.

It must have been about this hour that Charlie Stoddart's loon got his rabbits killed. They were stone cold by morning and their blood congealed. It is a wonder that Shinnie or the bobby didna see the foreman at the rabbit hutch. On the other hand, when Shinnie saw the bobby on to his bike at the head of the avenue it was easy for him to nip back thirty yards or so tae thrapple the craters, if he had a mind for it.

The foreman was summoned to appear in court. He was fined £5 and got his name in the papers. It was a month's pay and he had five bairns. He was never "socht tae bide" and his name was on every tongue in the district. For several months until the May term he had to carry on at Shinbrae, taking his orders from Shinnie and facing his workmates as if nóthing had happened, a hard thing in those days when men were jostling each other for a farmer's favours.

But there were some who despised Shinnie for his harsh treatment; dismissal was enough they said, without the fine. But Shinnie wanted to make an example of his victim, and every cottar at Shinbrae had to get rid of his hens.

Charlie Stoddart got over his 'flu and was soon back in the byre again. One evening his loon squared up beside Shinnie and watched his face.

"My rabbits are deid", he said, they wunna need nae mair neeps".

"Deid man! Whatever happened tae the craturs?"

"Somebody cut their throats!"

"Weel laddie, I tel't ye the foreman wad hae his ain back on ye for thrashin' his loon, though it was a damned sleekit wye

o' takin' his revenge. But he's had tae pay for't mair wyes than wan. And laddie," Shinnie went on, "never lat on, but when the foreman leaves at the term ye'll a' get yer hens back. I'll buy them at the roups and keep them or the term's by.
And maybe ye'll get up early the morn's mornin' and gie us a hand tae drive the nowt tae the station, there'll be a gie steer or we get them a' on the road."

PLAYING TRUANT

I sneezed in spite of myself and it almost proved my undoing. I sat very quiet in the drying loft over the kitchen where my father was at his dinner.

"Is that loon at the school the day?" I heard the old man ask.

"Of coorse he's at the school," mother lied, "what sorra made ye think that he wasna?"

"Och, I thocht I heard a soon!"

"Ach," mother scorned, "Ye're a muckle gipe, it's only the cat sneezin'. Sup yer broth man, and if ye are as hungry as ye usually are ye winna listen for ferlies."

So I sat very quiet, hoping that Flora, my little sister, wouldn't betray me. She was just at the stage when she might blurt out anything, and to warn her against it was like tempting her the more.

The skylight was a fixture, rusted with age and damp and curtained with cobwebs. Dry rot was crumbling the rafters and the floor-boards were porous with woodworm activity. There was dust and grime in every seam of the place, but also an atmosphere of romanticism and adventure which lent an air of bravado to my truancy.

It was in this loft that all my trophies were stored out of Flora's reach: my Hotspurs and Rovers, Sexton Blakes, Buffalo Bills, Nelson Lees, Comic Cuts and Comic Chips; cinema advertisements cut week by week from the newspapers, stacked high and neatly by the hatch where the ladder came up, and

19

all my cardboard cut-outs, soldiers, ships and motor cars;
it just wouldn't do to let Flora get her hands on these. And most
precious of all was my shoe-box theatre, with its aproned stage
and tiny chairs, the props and characters all set for a performance of "Mill O' Tifty's Annie." I had just seen the play
performed in the local hall and I was burning to have it done
in puppetry.

My old man fell asleep after his heavy meal and my behind
grew numb sitting on the hard floor boards. I felt like a Jack
on the Bean Stalk awaiting the Giant to awake from his snooze.
The old man was a heavy eater and to-day he had brose after
his usual dinner and it had sent him nearly into a coma.

When confronted with a normal meal the old man would
storm at mother about its lack of stamina. What would have
satisfied the appetite of most working men was no use to the
old man. "Some licht woman," he would screech, "some licht;
I canna work a yokin's wark on that — I'll need brose!"
So mother would set out the oat-meal bowl, salt and pepper,
and a jug of milk, and when the kettle came to the boil he
made brose. To-day had been no exception and I heard him
stirring his brose with the handle of his spoon. He always sat
bolt upright on the edge of his chair at meal times, and I could
picture it all quite plainly while I listened and waited.

And if it wasn't brose for dessert it was "melk and breid,"
oat-cakes warmed at the fire and crumbled into a bowl of milk,
sometimes with a dash of cream, sprinkled with pepper and
supped with a spoon, a tasty and invigorating diet, which I
sometimes shared with the old man.

I heard Flora come and rattle the door at the foot of the
loft stair. She had remembered for a moment where I was and
I held my breath in fear. But she went away again and all was
quiet.

Mother got the tea ready. I heard the tinkle of teaspoons
going into the cups.The old man had come to life again. I
heard the scrape of his chair on the cement floor as he
dragged it back to the table. He was preparing to face another
hard yokin' at the neep park and the coo byre and I knew he
did more than he was bargained for.

"Woman," says he, "see that the loon comes tae the byre the nicht: he could hash the neeps or cairry a pucklie strae — maybe gie the calves a sook, it's aye a help ye ken."

Mother was washing the dinner plates in a basin at the other end of the table.

"Oh aye," says she, "but ye maun gie the laddie time tae tak' his denner. He has tae travle a lang road frae the school. And never a copper does the fairmer gie 'im for his wark."

"But it's me he's helpin' woman, ye canna expect the fairmer tae pey him for that!"

"No no, but sometimes the fairmer trails the laddie awa' tae something else and he gets naething for that. He tak's the sap oot o' you but he's nae gaun tae tak' it oot o' the loon as weel. He'll hae tae work for a livin' when his day comes and surely that's time aneuch!"

"A' richt woman, but I'll be lookin' for 'im onywye. It's better than throwin' steens on the sklates or fleein' aboot wi' a gird. The laddie maun learn, woman!"

I heard the old man pushing his chair back from the table. I knew he would be putting on his sweaty cap and stroking mother's crow-black hair: "Ye're a bonnie crater though," he would purr, "aye are ye though."

"G'wa tae yer wark ye gock," I heard her say.

Then I heard the old man say a few silly childish words to Flora as he stepped over her dolls at the door.

I lifted the latch and descended the ladder into the lobby and the kitchen. The baker's van had been in the forenoon and I glanced at the table to see if there were any fancy pastries on the breadplate. Snatching a pancake, the only thing available, I sneaked to the door to see how far the old man had gone on the road. I had to do this because the water cistern blocked my view from the window. I couldn't see the old man from the door so I crept outside and peeped round the corner of the cistern.

Ah ha! too son! The old man was just entering the farm loanin' when he looked round and saw me. He shook his fist at me while I stood there like a fool with my mouth full of pancake.

He hadn't time to come back because it was too near yokin' time at the farm. Shaking his fist was all the malice he had resource to at the moment, but it was enough for me until nightfall when I could expect heavier punishment.

I ran back into the house and told mother.

"Weel weel," said she, as she wrung out her dishcloth, "Ye'll catch it when he comes home, and ye're supposed tae gyang tae the byre tae hash the neeps and feed the calfies. Ye should hae kept oot o' sicht a whilie langer."

"I wunna gyang tae the byre. He'll stab me wi' a fork like he tried the last time he was angered, the time he chased the foreman oot o' the byre."

I should have gone to the byre and softened the old man's wrath. But I cowered behind mother's skirts and hoped that she would stick up for me. And there was always the risk in the byre that the old man would take a fork over my back if he was thoroughly roused. Just the other day I had seen him chase the foreman out of the byre with a graip. Some tittle-tattle of evil gossip the foreman had spread around and it brought the old man into conflict with the other men.

"Spit it out!" I heard the foreman say, but he didn't wait for the old man to spit out anything, but ran like a schoolgirl when the old man charged him with the fork and well he may, for it was like a Highlander's charge at Prestonpans.

So I was in for it, and as the afternoon wore on my feeling of guilt grew stronger. From behind the window curtains I watched some of my classmates trudging home from school, boys and girls from outlying crofts, and the sight of them made me feel ashamed. It made me realise that I shouldn't play truant; that I should go to school like other respectable kids, and that I shouldn't deceive the old man, though mother let me off with it.

Mother lit the paraffin lamp and pulled down the blinds. She laid the supper plates on the table and took a bowl of meal out of the oak barrel to make the porridge.

I went up to the loft for my shoe-box and arranged it on

the dresser. "Mill O' Tifty's Annie" must go on at all costs. Flora was already seating her dolls around the stage to witness the performance. I had already done "Jamie Fleeman," and although the old man had snored through it all mother and Flora thought it was first class.

The old man had never thrashed me although I suppose I deserved it often enough. Once he had smacked my backside in a playful manner, under the bedclothes, and I had buried my face in the pillow with embarrassment because he could do this to me.

But now I could hear his footsteps outside on the gravel as he approached the door. Then he lifted the sneck and burst in upon us like a hungry bear....

"Fut wye was ye nae at the skweel?" His eyes were like hot pin-heads that burned into mine as I retreated before him to the meal-barrel in the corner.

He never even glanced at the table, which he usually did, whenever he opened the door, to see what was there for his ravenous belly. He fixed his searing eyes on my miniature theatre, stanced on the dresser, and with one swipe of his King-Kong arm he scattered the lot on the floor; stage, scenery, puppets, props and tiny chairs for my imaginary audience went flying under the table and over the fireplace.

That single action was symbolic of what he meant to do with my whole life. He seemed determined I should earn my bread the hard way, as he himself had done, and he had no respect whatsoever for any other inclinations I might have.

"D'ye ken I'm on my last warnin' for nae sendin' ye tae school? D'ye hear?" he roared, while I squeezed myself in behind the meal-barrel.

Frustration brought his anger to fever heat. He danced round the barrel in a frenzy, while little Flora hung on to the tail of his jacket, trying to pull him away. He wrenched her off and sent her spinning into a corner, where she sat on her doup, howling, with hot tears on her cheeks.

"D'ye want me tae stand in jile for ye? Ye damned rascal!" And he lashed out at me with his open hand.

The blow toppled me out from behind the meal barrel and

sent me rolling over the floor. He was on me in a moment and I crawled under the table to escape his groping hands.

Now he was thoroughly roused and began chasing me round the table, first one side and then the other, and all the time I dodged him, while he stretched out his arm to prevent me reaching the door.

The table began to rock, rattling the cups in their saucers and spilling the milk from the porridge bowls. This nettled mother and she flew at the old man like a tigress, dragging him away from me by the jacket.

"Ye senseless fool," she screamed, "What sort o' wye is that tae carry on in the hoose? Folk wad think ye was mad!" And when the old man turned on her I bolted for the door.

He raised his arm to strike her but she grabbed the poker from the fender and dared him to try it. Her eyes gleamed with defiance and her lips quivered on set teeth.

The old man lowered his fist. "Oh aye," he yelled, "Ye'll tak' his bludy pairt will ye, and hae me stand the jile? Ye're spoilin' 'im as it is. He'll never do a stroke o' wark when his day comes. But mind I'm tellin' ye he's nae gyan tae lie aboot here in idleness. He'll hae tae work for a livin' the same as I did afore his day. I'll see that he does it. You wait and see!"

Mother shook the poker in his face and his eyes wavered confronting her.

"Gyang tae yer supper man and lat the loon alane. You keep yer hands tae yersel and I'll see that he goes tae school."

"But woman, it wunna dee at a'! Can't ye see I'm on my last warnin? And what wad become o' ye a' if I gaed tae jile?"

"Ach, awa' man, ye're saft; they'll never send ye tae prison. They juist say that tae scare ye!"

So the old man cooled off and sat down to his porridge, now getting cold with a skin on top, so he didn't have to blow on the spoon, and it humoured him a little.

I sneaked inside from the cold to gather up my theatre. Flora gave me a hand, her great soft eyes swimming in tears and her golden curls glistening on her shoulders. The stage had been buckled in the scuffle and the scenery squashed and scattered, but we managed to arrange it somehow.

After supper Flora re-arranged her dolls on a chair in front of the stage. I had painted a fine back-drop in watercolour of the old Mill of Tifty, with a model of the waterwheel in front, and when I brought Bonnie Annie and Andrew Lammie on to the stage Flora gave a little gasp of delight.

And then I began my soliloquy:

"At Mill o' Tifty lived a man
In the neighbourhood of Fyvie,
Who had a lovely daughter fair ——
Her name was Bonnie Annie .... "

But the old man was asleep, bolt upright on a hard chair, his head hanging over the back, his mouth agape, snoring.

He never did really understand me.

RAB O' THE BARNYARDS

Character Study Of A North-East Worthy.

The Barnyards was a muckle sair toon tae work on. Man and
beast were chauved on her lang clay rigs. He was a tearin'
brute Rab Imray that was the grieve, a big chiel that could
have been a bobby, but he took a bit wife and cottared at
the Barnyards. Rab was in his late thirties, six feet lang, well
built, with black curly hair, tawny complexion, a mouser and
brown dancing eyes. He wore a pickiesae hat, a muffler, a
sleeved waistcoat, Kersey-tweed trousers, tackety boots and
nicky-tams.
    It was a modern fairm for the times, with electric light,
milking machines, attested cows in concrete stalls — and even
a tractor, a muckle traction-engine o' a thing that stinkit the
the barn and foonert in the neep park and never did any good
at all. There were six cottars and two single lads in the
bothy. Three of the men were horsemen, two were stockmen,
one was an orraman, while another drove the milk lorry and
washed the cans and milk bottles.
    It was hard times, no family allowance, no dole; the work
was hard, the hours long and labour was cheap. It was a period
that bred men like Rab of the Barnyards; rough, hardy,
eident chiels, the likes of whom will never be seen on the farms
again. They knew nothing of half-holidays, summer holidays
or paid overtime. Their work was their lives and they made a
song of the grindstone of life.
    Rab had full charge, second only to the Barnyards himsel',
and he worked the odd pair of horse, off and on, when he wasn't

26

pu'in' neeps — usually a pair of raw colts that nobody else could handle. But Rab soon had them tamed with his long strides ahin the harras, or in the muckle stone roller that was for crushing the clods, for they were by-ordinar at the Barnyards. In the spring, when the grun was made, the creatures were as thin they could have loupit through their collars. Their shoulders were blistered with the strain of the yoke and they had to rest in the stable or they healed. Losh aye, Rab was sair on horse, and while the creatures were convalescent he tore at the neeps or the muck himsel' like one demented.

When they emptied the dung court with the horse carts the cottar lads had their wives come up with a drop tea through the yokin'. But Rab wadna tak' tea, "Na, na," says he, "I've heard o' a bairn needin' a piece, but nae a grown body. I'll easy fill 'er wantin' tae." And he tore at the muck with a shoulder pick and loaded it in graipfuls that nae mortal body was fit for.

Rab and the first horseman lived next door and their wives couldna gree. They spat at each other like cats and were itchin' tae get at the ither's hair, each kyarding the other from the door jamb. The foreman's wife had sax bairns. She was a thrifty body and made a' their claes hersel', while Rab's wife could hardly thread a needle. But it made Rab's wife jealous and filled her with envy and she couldna stand the look o' the woman.

But Rab got on capital with his foreman, a lang teem whaup with freckles and a red heid. They never spoke about their wives or their bairns but kept the peace like decent folk, and never entered the other's door. And the foreman would say to Rab: "Man, I need a hair-cut," and Rab would take his clipper to the stable, and the foreman would sit on a box with a saddle-cover round his shoulders, and Rab would shear off his red hair like wool from a ram. "Fine deen man!" the foreman would say; then Rab sat on the box and the foreman took his turn with the clipper.

The Barnyards himsel' was a hard maister folk said. Woe betide a poor cottar if he was fee-ed to go to the Barnyards. "Rab will tak' the sap oot o' the breet!" And maybe he did, the slavin' brute, but you didn't do it for nothing. Rab saw to that. And if the Barnyards had been a bit grippie wi' the bawbees Rab made it up wi' merchandise.

But if the Barnyards was a hard master he was also a tolerant one. And sometimes he said nasty things to his servants that Rab didn't hear, and maybe just as well, or Rab would have him by the lug. But tons of coal went missing at the Barnyards, loads of firewood, gallons of milk and the finest cream — they even took the man's paraffin and diesel oil to light their fires, and a hantle other petty theft that the Barnyards closed his eyes to. He knew all right but he never locked a door, and Rab carried the keys for the loft and the engine-hoose. But if you pleased Rab; if you could keep up with Rab in the neep park, or in the dung court, then you had nothing to fear from the Barnyards. Coal was a perquisite (part of the wages) and if it was exhausted before the winter term Rab would have the foreman yoke a horse-cart before daybreak and they would fill half-a-dozen sacks from the farm coalshed. And while it was still dark the horsemen would cart it round the starving cottars and dump a bag on every doorstep.

One day at the marts a neighbour said to the Barnyards: "Man, I dinna ken fut wye ye keep Rab Imray yonder as a grieve; he's sic a lad tae steal!"

"Aye, I ken Rab steals," said the Barnyards, "but man, he's worth it!"

And so he was, for Rab got more work out of his men than though he had been thoroughly a farmer's man, with no thought for his workers. They slaved behind him in all sorts of weather without complaint. Though other folks were taking in their tattie-boodies from the wet Rab and his squad were still drabbling on at the hoe. Has the man no pity, folk would ask each other from their stable doors: but the neeps were in a blaze of growth and Rab wanted them singled before they got harder to do, for they were shooting up with every blink of sun between the thunder pelts.

For nigh on twelve years Rab had farmed the Barnyards. Never had its yields been so high, or its soil in such fertility. "If ye can grow grass," said Rab, "and bury a good sole, you'll farm the Barnyards."

28

If it were a sunny evening in the spring you could see Rab in his sark-sleeves striding on ahin the turnip-sower, to catch a favourable break in the weather. The horsemen had set up the drills in the daytime, still with a dry loam to take seed, and Rab meant to have them all sown before dark. And if you looked again before bed-time Rab was still at it, his mare lathered in foam, the drills all flattened behind him like corduroy.

When the Barnyards had his breeks off, ready for bed, he took the curtain aside on the storm window and saw Rab in the neep park. "Aye Bess," he said, looking at his wife, "I ken ye dinna like Rab, and I ken he steals — but whaur wad I get his marra?"

And if you leaned over the dyke and asked Rab the reason for his hurry he would stroke his fusker and his eyes would dance all over your face. "Man," he would say, "there's naething here but clay and watter. Ye've got tae catch 'er in the mood for seed or ye'll never see a neep or the simmer's gaen; a' droon't wi' watter or hang't wi' hard clay."

And if Rab "took a tig" in the hairst time he would yoke a binder and cut a whole park of corn on a Sunday and never ask a penny for it. The hairst was sometimes finished at the Barnyards, and the stacks all thatched, first in the district. And at the marts a neighbour would say to the Barnyards: "Aye man, ye've feenished!"

"Aye," says the Barnyards, "we're throu. Rab took a tig, the breet!"

Now the Barnyards had a cow that took the red-water, and when the vet ordered that two crates of stout be given to her, Rab and the dairymen had their daily pint for a fortnight. When the cow died Rab said: "Ach weel, the cooie was gaun tae dee onywye. It wad hae been a shame tae conach the gweed stuff on a dyin' beastie!"

Rab and the dairymen understood each other perfectly, a rare coincidence on most dairy farms. There were few complaints about "frostet neeps' or "foostie strae" if Rab could help it, and the only time they ever emptied the barn they came upon an old horse-gig under the straw that even the Barnyards couldn't remember.

And sometimes on a rainy day you would see Rab and his men with the horse-clipper in the byre, taking turns at the handle, helping the bailies to shear their cows. Rab was a dab hand with the clipper, snaking it under a cow's belly from the long tube on the machine, fondling her teats as canny as if it were a woman's breasts. "It wad be a bittie akward gaen the women had them here!" he would drawl, and the billies would laugh their agreement. But the cottars went home with their flaggons brimming with milk. Even their cats had something to thank Rab for.

Old Bess of the Barnyards didn't like Rab. Maybe she had good reason, for her hens took such a fancy to Rab that sometimes they laid their eggs in his pockets. "Man," Rab would joke, "I can hardly hang my jacket on an aul' roostie nail somewye but there's a hennie lays in my pooches!"

Rab's hens never moulted as far as the grocer was concerned; His basket was about the same level all the year round. Nor was he slack to thraw a hen's neck for the Sunday dinner, especially if he saw her blinking her eyes in a corner, standing there as if she were in a trance, and maybe only needing the rooster. Sometimes the creatures sat down at his touch, as a hen will do in such a mood, but if Rab were in need of a dinner it were better for her that she had flown over the steading.

Bess couldn't risk leaving a fish to dry on the hake by the kitchen door or some lousy cottar would be off with it overnight. She had to lock the meat safe and empty the cheese-press if Rab was on the prowl. And the salt herrin' barrel was a sore temptation.

She was a great horticulturist was Bess, the mistress of the Barnyards. She had a great notion of trees and shrubs and such like, and took great pride in her lawns and flower gardens. But when she rose one morning she missed a certain tree from the farm avenue. She looked from her oriel window, high on the slated roof, and behold — the tree was gone!

Bess called to the Barnyards, who was still in his bed, and got him over to the window, where she pointed to the gap in the loanin.

"That's Rab done that I'll be damned!" she cried. "That's

yer grieve you are so daft on!"

The Barnyards stood wheezing at the pane; it was a chest
complaint that troubled him, off and on, and he shivered in
his nightgown. "Ach woman," says he, "what aboot a tree,
it couldna been a big ane. Ye'll see the road better withoot
it!"

"It was a beech," she shouted, "one o' the first tae bud in
the spring. But I'll search every cottar's coalhouse on the place
or I find it!"

And so she did, and found the tree in Rab's coalshed, all
sawn into slabs, ready for the hack-block, and the branches in a
heap at the gable. And Bess gave Rab's wife a tinking, in front
of the foreman's wife and the bairns, and the poor woman was in
tears, all for Rab's sake at the ploo.

Bess went back to the farmhouse, where she found the
Barnyards in the parlour. "Ye'll sack that man this very day!"
she cried.

"Poor Rab," wheezed the Barnyards, sair chauved for
breath. "But I'll do no such thing woman. Nae for the sake o' a
blastet tree! Rab is a kleptomaniac; he canna help stealin'
Can't ye understand, woman?"

"I can understand a' richt, but that doesna mean that you
should be his nursemaid. A merry dance he leads them all, a
wonder he doesna have ye oot at the door. The place is hardly
yer ain man, they cottars are takin' possession!"

"I'll survive woman. Rab's worth every penny he steals, aye
and mair. The wages I can affoord tae pay them doesna gie
the cottar bairns justice onywye!"

They argued about it for the rest of the day and it ended in
a sulk between them.

Because of his complaint the Barnyards wasn't allowed to
smoke, doctor's orders, and Bess watched him with a ferret's
eye. So about supperin' time in the evening he put on his
carpets and went down the close to see Rab.

Some of the lads might be brushing harness on the cornkists,
or shaking chains in a sack to make them shine; but Rab had no
such capers, for anything did with the colts, all the old harness,
and some of it was tied together with bits of wire. He had a

little stable all by himself, where he was grooming his colts by electric light when the Barnyards wheezed in at the door.

"Aye Rab," says he. "Aye man," says Rab, and banged his steel comb against the travis post. The post was poke-marked with years of banging to knock the dust out of Rab's comb.

A long pause ensued and the the the Barnyards cleared his throat. "Man Rab," says he, "what aboot a draw o' yer pipe?"

"Fairlie man," says Rab, and he filled his pipe with black twist and lit it and gave it to his master. And the old man puffed and wheezed fair in his element.

"Man Rab," says he, "that's grand!"

There was another long silence. The scrape of iron teeth on horse hair. The rattle of a manger chain. The munch and scent of hay. Cosy. A haven of peace for the Barnyards. The tension of the day had left him and he was relaxed; even his breathing was easier and there was less of a heave in his chest.

"It was a beech, Rab?"

"Aye."

"Grand burnin' Rab?"

"Aye."

The Barnyards sighed and handed back the pipe. "For God's sake Rab, whatever else ye steal keep it oot o' sicht o' the mistress!" And when Rab looked out the door he was gone in the darkness.

Somebody said to Rab that he might get disease letting the Barnyards smoke his pipe. "Fie man," says Rab, "the pipe may kill the Barnyards, but there's nae a germ born that wad live in my pipe!" And they said that if you stood beside Rab in a mornin' when he smoked it you could believe him.

But there was a change at the Barnyards. One of Rab's men left for a cairter's job in the toon, and a young chiel newly married took his place. Rab put a sod on his lum and smoked his young bride out of the house her first mornin' at the Barnyards. "We had tae get a look at the crater," says Rab. "I thocht it was the best wye tae get 'er ootside. Lucky she was we didna wash her feet as weel. There's nae scarcity o' harness blaik and cairt grease."

But he was a saft stock the new lad; fair scared at the Barnyards and feart at a' the thievin' that gaed on. Bein' newly married he didn't have to steal. Most of the older cottars had big families. They had to steal to keep them alive. And besides, if you didn't steal something at the Barnyards you was laughed at. If you had offered to pay the Barnyards for a bushel of corn for your hens he would have been dumbfounded. The cottars got their corn when the mill choked on thrashin' days. Rab never swept the barn floor, he left that for the cottars. "Tidy it up at supperin' time lads," he would say, "it'll do for yer hens. Losh aye, the hennies like forty-twa pun corn, nae neen o' yer sma' dirt!"

But the new chiel tried hard to be honest. Fegs aye, hardly took a neep for his broth or a bit stick to light his fire. But he couldna buy kindling anywhere, the stock, at ony price, and he was fair stuck for tinder. In the lang run he had to confide in Rab. So one evening in the barn Rab went up to the loft for an old wooden bushel that was falling apart anyway. He threw it down at the man's feet in the barn, where it went all to staves. "Noo than," says Rab, with a wink to the other lads, "that'll be a start for ye. The iron hoops winna burn, but ye can try yer luck wi' the timmer bitties!"

So the new lad gathered up his staves in a chorus of ridicule. To leave them would have angered Rab, the last thing he wanted, but he felt he had paid well enough for his honesty.

It was a tonic to watch Rab start the oil-engine when he was going to thrash or bruise corn for the beasts: filling the glass jars with oil over the piston, topping up the cooling tank with water from the horse-trough, priming and lighting the blow-lamp.

When the nose cone was red hot Rab twisted the great black fly-wheels this way and that. The engine gave a pech, spat and said "Ach! Nae the day!"

"Thrawn bitch!" Rab seched.

But he persisted and spun the wheels again. The engine gave a hoast, then a bark and back-fired, and threw Rab nearly out at the door, muckle brute though he was.

"Stand back lads," cried Rab, his eyes fair dancin', "there's life in 'her yet!"

The piston gave a lurch or two and the black greasy thing sprang into vibrating life, spinning the wheels at such a spate ye couldna see the spokes.

Rab liked to have her chookin' afore yokin' time, to be ready for the lads. He slipped the mill belt on to the pulley and the stripper drum picked up speed till it hummed in its velocity. Rab jumped into the feed box and opened the lid on the drum, gave his knife a bit scrape on the harled wall and fastened it on his wrist, ready for the sheaves from the foreman's fork. Then look out, as he cut the bands on the sheaves to the drum, for if you wasn't smothered in dust you was nearly buried in straw.

Rab was coming home at the gloamin' with a pail of water in one hand and a bucket of milk in the other (not a flaggon mind you — which was all he was entitled to) but an open pail, brimming with goodness.

Now at this time the cottars carried their water from the steading. Some of them had a bowie 'neath the spoot at the gable, to catch a suppie rain water from the roof, mostly for washing, but they carried their cooking water in pails from the Barnyards.

And Rab met a lad wi' a hat in the avenue, an insurance mannie or something, and he fair glowered at Rab and his twa pails. And when Rab saw that the mannie kent what was in the off-side pail he says, sober like: "Jod man, the verra taps are runnin' melk at the Barnyards. I juist held tee ma pail and that's what I got!" But the mannie just nodded his heid and passed on.

But the mannie wasna sae blate as Rab thocht he was. He kent fine it was the cooler tap in the dairy that Rab meant, where he'd no business to be, except that the water tap was beside it. Rab could have said that he mistook the taps, just as cool as he would have told you that the sea was on fire, hoping that you would believe it.

But nobody was any the wiser, nobody that mattered. The mannie never lat dab to the Barnyards. He had his custom to collect and maybe he didn't want to give his name an ill taste with the cottars.

But in the winter of that year tragedy struck at Rab and his

34

wife. They lost their youngest son of four years, struck down with some rare disease that the doctors couldn't fathom. Rab stood at the graveside with big tears on his cheeks, great glistening drops that slid down his face and hung at his mouser. You could hardly believe that Rab could greet, him that was always so cheerful and made a joke of life. But he had come to it at last and his great shoulders shook with his sobbing. Those who shook hands with Rab that day had never seen him in such a state.

Rab's moustache had a droop after this, and sometimes the dancing eyes were wet with tears. When you came upon him canny like, when his thoughts were deep, you could see it had been a sair day for Rab when his son died.

Old Bess even softened her heart to Rab in his grief. For a time she settled her differences with the Barnyards about Rab the grieve.

But Rab took a thinking, for his wife was sair come at in their sorrow, and when feeing time came round Rab thought a change of scene might help her.

Folks fair thocht that Rab would be leaving the Barnyards 'cause he hadna put a spade to his gairden that spring. And when he lit his pipe there was a shake in his hands 'hat wasn't there before.

But the Barnyards went down the close in his carpets again to Rab's little stable. Between puffs at Rab's pipe he said: "Ye'll be bidin' on again Rab?"

"Na, nae this time," says Rab, "the wife's sair come at. She needs a change."

"Ye're nae wunnin awa' onywye. I'll raise ye a fiver for the year and I'll tak' yer wife aboot in the car. She'll get a the change o' scenery whe wants withoot flittin' for't!"

Rab hummed and hawed and twirled his mouser. "Weel weel," says he, "I'll see what the wife says."

So for a time Rab's wife went everywhere with the Barnyards, and it fair took her out of herself. But now it was the foreman's wife that was jealous and she taunted Rab's wife about taking up with the Barnyards, an old man that could nearly be her father. But when folks saw Rab's wife chase the woman back to her ain door with a sweeping brush they said she was fair cured of her melancholia.

But a day came at last for the Barnyards poor stock and he became really ill. Rab asked for the maister once or twice but was never allowed at his bedside. When he died Rab knew that his ain time would no be lang at the Barnyards. He knew that Bess would be rid of him at the next May Term, so he looked for another place that suited him. Nor was the Barnyards long under the sod or Bess had a great cumbersome stone set up on top of him. "Just tae mak' sure he doesna interfere in her wyes," Rab said, with some of his old good humour returning; "losh aye, yon muckle steen will fairly hud 'im doon."

So Bess got rid of Rab at the May Term, and all the rabble of cottars that did his every bidding. "She wants a clean toon lads," Rab said to his men, "we'll a' hae tae go!"

"I wadna like a woman boss onywye," Rab concluded. "I've ane at hame already; anither ane at my wark wad be hell upon earth."

TOUCH AND GO!

It was a dark winter's night that Wee Tam's mither and Mrs.
Lunan, a neighbour body, planned a raid on a nearby farmer's
henhouse. Mrs. Lunan's man was a cripple, and they lived in
an old croft house down in the howe of Glenshinty. They had
three or four bairns running barefoot around the place, with
hardly a stitch of clothing on their backs, but somehow they
managed to scrape along on a mere pittance from the Assistance
Board, and once in a while the Inspector of the Poor looked in
by to see if the creatures were still alive.

"Ma man's been real poorly lately," said Mrs. Lunan, warming
her hands at the fire, "and a drappie o' chicken bree wad do
him a world o' good."

"But whaur are we gaun tae get a hen at this time o' nicht?"

"Steal ane!" cried Tam's mither, and she looked at the
woman half in sympathy, half in fear, wondering what she was
going to say next.

"Aye, we'll try auld Grimshaw's place; it's fine near the road
and naebody wad jalouse us there. Get on yer coat wife and gie
us a hand."

"A' richt wifie, but it's a bit risky," said Tam's mither,
buttoning up her coat; "and Tam, put on yer bonnet and come
and watch the coast is clear for us, and see there's nae ferlies
aboot."

Wee Tam shut his book and shuddered. He had been reading
"Robinson Crusoe," a big book that he had got from the
dominie, one of those old-fashioned editions with beautifully

stencilled capitals at the beginning of each chapter, and with
a short summary of the events therein related. The loon was just
getting fully absorbed in this pirate and cutlass masterpiece when
the women hatched their plan.

The lamp was lit and the blinds were down and Tam's father
snored in the box-bed. He was an early bedder and missed much
of the goings on in the hoose, but Tam felt that the old man had
one eye open half the time and that he listened between the
snores. But he never interfered, mither was boss. Flora, Tam's
little sister, lay snugly at her father's back, curled like a buckie,
a doll in her oxter, and Tam felt it was a pity he hadn't gone to
bed, then perhaps the women wouldn't have bothered him.

It was inky black and bitter cold outside. A mass of stars
spangled the sky, and Tam could pick out the Seven Sisters
twinkling above the dark smudge of pinewood on the Berry
Hill. But apart from the sough and flap of the wind the world
was as silent as a graveyard.

Tam shivered in his thin jacket as he trudged on behind the
women, trying to identify the adventure with what he had been
reading in Robinson Crusoe. About a mile along the road they
came to Grimshaw's place, a big croft by the roadside, which
Tam passed every day going to school. There was a lean-to
poultry shed at the gable of the steading, close by the road,
but in full view of the kitchen door.

The women first went past the farmhouse, to make sure
there were no lights in the windows, walking on the grass to
quieten the sound of their footsteps, then came back to where
Tam waited at the henhouse.

Tam watched and listened but nobody stirred, nothing but
the faint smell of the sharn midden and the scent of stale peat
smoke that came to his nostrils on the wind. Everybody was
asleep at this hour so the two women crept into the henhouse.
They groped for a couple of good plump birds on the roost
and wrung their necks before a cackle escaped them. There
was some flapping of wings and a flutter of feathers when
they came out, but never a squawk from the dead birds.
They put the hens in a sack, closed the hen-house door and
made off, Wee Tam behind them, still walking on the grass,

all as silent as doomsday.

Safely home Tam went back to Robinson Crusoe Island, thinking no more about the affair, glad to be back to the fire and the lamplight, snug in the satisfaction that he could read till his eyes closed without further interruption, for it was just past midnight.

The women set to plucking the hens in the kitchen, while the birds were still warm, which makes it easier to do, and cleaning them, getting them ready for the dinner, maybe with a plate of broth first and the hen to follow, but Mrs. Lunan said she would roast hers because she wanted the "bree' for her sick man.

Tam got a helping when he got home from school, running all the way at the thought of it, his satchel unstrapped and under his arm, to save the thump of it on his back. And it had been a rare treat, especially the stuffing and the white flesh around the breast-bone, which mither had laid aside for him, and his old man had never asked where the hen came from.

In the evening, after supper, Tam was lighting a cigarette over the lamp glass on the kitchen table, when the local bobby laid his bicycle against the unblinded window. Tam quickly snibbed the fag in the fire, just as the bobby walked in, never waiting for an answer to his knock on the door.

"Aye lad," says the bobby, as he peeled off his leather gloves, "I fairly caught ye that time. I suppose ye ken that sixteen is the age for smokin'."

Tam squeezed himself into the corner behind the meal barrel, his surest refuge in times of trouble. He remembered the hen in the dresser and he felt terribly guilty and afraid. His father was seated by the fireside. The policeman turned to him and said: "Don't ye know it's illegal for the lad tae smoke afore he's sixteen?"

Tam's father scratched his balding head, tired from his day's work in the byres. "Oh aye," says he, wearily, "but the laddie gie's me a hand in the byre, and for that I dinna grudge 'im a bit blaw at a fag."

But the bobby was indignant' "It's not a question of whether you can afford it man, but you're breaking the law!" He turned to Tam's mither, who was placing a chair for him — "Woman," he said, "do ye allow this to go on the hoose: the rascal smokin' and him still at school?"

"Oh aye, but the man's boss in the hoose here," she lied, thankful that the tiny wish-bone from the hen was in the oven, and not on the crook over the range as it might have been. When it became thoroughly brittle Tam would share it with his little sister: each would take a splint of it in the crook of a little finger, make a wish and pull, and whoever had the broken end when the bone snapped would lose the wish.

The constable sat down on a hard chair in the middle of the cement floor, crossed his legs and laid his "cheese-cutter" cap on his knee. He was so near the hen now he could have smelled it. He only had to reach over to open the dresser door and there was the skeleton of it, on a plate.

He was much nearer Tam's height on the varnished chair and the loon breathed a little more freely behind the meal barrel. Nevertheless he was still a mighty giant in the shabby little kitchen, his red face polished with stern authority and his silver buttons twinkling in the lamplight. Tam focused his attention on the bobby's putteed leg, which he kept swinging up and down over his knee, as if he wished to show off the highly polished boot at the end of it, a boot that would give you a hefty kick in the buttocks if he got near enough.

"Have ye seen ony strange characters in the vicinity?" the bobby asked, looking first at Tam's mither, and then at his father. "Auld Sandy Grimshaw has missed some hens out of his shed, and says that by the mess of feathers ootside the door, he feels sure they have been stolen."

Tam's father suddenly recalled his splendid dinner but swallowed the thought. "No," he said, trying to look unconcerned, "no, we hinna seen a crater, not a crater!"

Tam's mither poured out a glass of Dr. Watson's Tonic Stout for the bobby, and one for her husband. It was the only hop beverage in the house and she excelled in the brewing of it, though she sometimes made broom wine in the summer, with a taste like whisky.

"Ye ken auld Grimshaw's place?" the bobby asked, taking the

glass in his fat, beringed fingers.

"Aye," said Tam's mither, wiping her hands on her apron, "I ken the fairm: it's at the top o' the quarry brae, nae far frae the shop."

"Aye, ye ken wuman, I'm nae supposed tae drink in uniform, but in this case we'll mak' an exception."

"Ach man, that stuff will never touch ye!" And Tam's mither busied herself wiping the table of what she had spilled, for the bottles were brisk and the froth had hit the roof when she removed the corks.

Tam's wee sister came forward with her biggest doll and laid it on the bobby's knee. He bent the doll forward in his huge hand and it "Ba-a-a-ed" pitifully, as if it had a tummy ache. He only had to ask little Flora what Dolly had for dinner and he had the case wrapped up.

But the local flat-foot was no Sherlock Holmes, and he believed only what he saw; like loons smoking while still in short breeks, or a poor farm servant chauving home against the wind without a rear-light on his bicycle.

Otherwise there wasn't a feather of evidence in sight. The wing feathers were tied in a bundle in the cubby-hole under the loft stair. Tam's mither would wash them and use them to brush her oat-cakes before she put them on the girdle over the fire. The downs were concealed in a sack; she would stuff them into a pillow after they had been fumigated. The cats had eaten all the offal on the midden. There wasn't a shred of evidence left anywhere in sight.

The bobby licked his lips and set the empty glass on the table. "Thanks mistress," he said, wiping his moustache, "that was capital!"

He got up and put on his peaked cap and gloves, glowering down at wee Tam behind the meal barrel. "Ye can coont yersel' lucky lad," he said, "lucky that I'm nae takin' ye tae the lock-up. Gin yer mither hadna been sic a gweed-he'rtet wuman, and yer faither sic an honest decent body, I might hae run ye in for smokin'. But if I catch ye at it again I wunna be sae lenient!"

Turning to Tam's mither in the door he said: "Bye the by

mistress, wha bides in that hoose in the howe, alang the Laich Road?"

"Oh," says Tam's mither, wondering what the bobby was leading to, "It's Mrs. Lunan bides there."

The bobby was now outside on the gravel, his brass buttons shining in the light from the open doorway, for it was now quite dark. "Mrs. Lunan," says he, still quizzical, "and do ye think she wad hae seen onybody suspicious, or could gie us ony information?"

Tam's mither began to tremble with excitement. "Oh I hardly think so," she said, trying to seem unconcerned, "she's a bittie frae the road and disna see mony strangers."

"Ah weel," replied the bobby, "but I'd better look in and see her onywye. Gweed nicht Mistress!"

The policeman was scarcely astride his bicycle when Mrs. Lunan burst in on Tam's folk from the darkness. They had been watching the rear-light on the bobby's bike as he sped down the brae. All had seemed lost but now they crowded round Mrs. Lunan in the lighted doorway, to see what could be done.

"Run wifie," cried Tam's mither, exasperated, "fly hame as fast as ye can, the bobby has been here and he's just left, and he's on the road tae your hoose noo. Run wifie, for heaven's sake run!"

"Michty mee!" cried the woman, "I meant tae borrow something, but that doesna matter noo. Michty mee! oor hen's still on the table, or what's left o't!" And away she flew, clambering over the dyke like a schoolgirl, lost in the darkness.

It was touch and go: the bobby on his bike round by the road, the woman on her feet across the wet fields. The bobby had a few minutes start ahead of her and she had another dyke to jump, and a deep ditch lay in her path.

Wee Tam could see the bobby's light as he moved along the Laich Road, but he could only guess how the woman fared in the darkness. The bobby had a gate to open at the end of the cart-track that led to the cottage. Tam closed the lobby door to shut in the light and waited. It wouldn't do to let the bobby know they were watching. It was touch and go ...

It was close on midnight when Mrs. Lunan went panting back to Tam's mither with the news. "Michty mee," she gasped, "I got hame first but just in time. It was a near thing I can tell ye. I was like tae faint and fair oot o' breath or I reached the door. I put the hen oot o' sight in the dresser, double quick. I just had time tae get my breath back when the bobby rapped on the door. I closed the lobby door so's he couldna see my face in the licht, and he never cam' ben the hoose, so he never noticed my weet shoes and stockin's. Thank heavens he didna find us oot. We wunna hae tae try that again wifie!"

Tam's mither was relieved. "Na faith ye," she said, ' but how's yer man Mrs. Lunan?"

"He's fine," said the woman, "but he doesna ken a thing aboot it. He's sound asleep and he thinks I bocht the hen, me that hardly has a copper penny tae clap on anither."

Tam's mither gave her a brimming glass of Dr. Watson's Tonic Stout: "Just to cheer you up wifie," as she said, while the froth flew from the uncorked bottle.

Wee Tam went back to the lamp glass and relit his cigarette. His old man had gone to bed but he stopped snoring immediately and raised himself on his elbow, blinking at the light. "Ony tae wuman?" says he, looking at his wife. "No I dinna want the stout, nae at this time o' nicht, juist a drap tae. So that was whaur the hen cam' frae, auld Grimshaw. Weel weel, she was a tasty bird onywye!"

And then he turned on Wee Tam, now seated on a kitchen

chair with "Robinson Crusoe," the fag reek rising above the open pages. "But ye'll hae tae watch yer smokin' ma loon, and if ye dinna come tae the byre when I want ye I'll tell the bobby ye've been at it again, ye wee rascal!"

The old blackmailer, Tam thought, but it should have taught the women a lesson.

KNOWIE'S MIDDEN LICHT.

Auld Knowie lived by the clock. He carried a gold watch with a
lid on its face, fastened to his waistcoat by a thin chain. In the
stable at noon, waiting for yoking time, he took the bit watch
out of his pocket and flicked the lid open, watching the hands
as they approached the hour. Several times he did this, and if
you had been the fee-ed lad at the Knowehead you would have
noticed that when he closed the lid with a final snap the hour
had come.

And you would wait for Knowie's orders like he was an
army captain, and then you would grab a saddle and throw it
on your horse's back like you was in the mounted cavalry,
for Knowie was a great lad for discipline and he liked to have
you lined up at the drinking trough on the stroke of one.

But for all his barking his bite wasn't as sharp as some folk
would say, and his line-up at the horses' trough wasn't all that
impressive, especially if you had come from a three or four-
paired place, for Knowie had only one pair of horse and an
orra-beast, worked by his son, young Knowie yonder that
was foreman, and a bit nipper of a loon he had fee-ed for the
odd beast and to help with the kye.

And if you had never been to jail six month's in Knowie's
chaumer would have given you a fairly good idea of what it would
be like. All this yammer about the good old bothy days is just
a lot of white-wash and the sooner you was married the better
if you wanted a decent kip. Not that Knowie could help this;
he wasn't to be blamed for the chaumer being biggit over the

midden, and it was no worse and no better than any other you had lived in. But you would get no fire in Knowie's chaumer, except on your Sunday as "Toon Keeper," every third week-end, looking after the kye and the horse, and maybe it was for fear you set fire to the steading, you being but a cottar bairn and not supposed to have as much wit as decent folk. And while Knowie's kye could lie down in brilliant electric light you had to go to sleep with a leaking paraffin lamp, so they had to trust you with that because there was no light in your bothy, which made you of less importance socially than the nowt in Knowie's byre.

Your chaumer was part of the hay-loft above the stable, with only a thin partition between you and the hay-seed, and damned if you could have slept for the stamping of iron hoofs on the cobblestones, or for the rattle of manger chains or the scamper of rats at the corn kists. And there was no such thing as a wardrobe, so you hung your Sunday clothes on to rusty nails hammered into the partition, and the hay-worms came wriggling through the seams and lost themselves in the pockets of your best suit.

How would you like to be standing at the top of the Broadgate, in the Town Square, having a bit crack with some of your cronies and a hay-worm looking through your buttonhole? He had taken a night's lodgings under the lapel of your jacket, and the heat of your body had made him seek a breath of fresh air, so he wriggles to your buttonhole and sticks his head out to see who you are talking to, and if it happened to be your favourite kitchiedeem, and her a bit squeamish, it would maybe be the last you would see of her. So you would seize the "crawlin' ferlie" with thoom and fore-finger and throw him on the pavement and squash him with your heel, while your deem would giggle or look the other way, depending on her mentality. So you would curse Knowie and his hay-worms and wish for the term, especially if it had cost you your best quine.

Knowie's chaumer had the usual wooden bed which looked like part of the building, and it was fitted with bottom boards and a chaff tick. Some folk called them "tikes", which were merely two sheets of linen sewn together like a great big sack and stuffed with chaff. They were bought in the shops ready to

45

fill, bed-size and mostly white with red or blue stripes, and they served as a mattress for farmer and cottar, a cosy one at that, and when it was newly filled you had to loup on a chair to get into bed. But Knowie himself maybe had a hair mattress by now, or even a feather bed like the gentry; for seeing he was so far ahead with everything else this wasn't likely to be overlooked for his comfort.

Being a young chiel with the blood of youth in your body you had no need of a hot-water bottle, but if you had been an old frail creature and asked for such a thing at the Knowehead you would have been laughed at, for while you was shut out at night with the horses and the nowt beasts all the others were coddled in the farmhouse. So you would have stood a poor chance if you had been an old body at the Knowehead, for more than likely you would have hoasted your hinder-end or died of chronic bronchitis before anyone noticed you was a human being like the rest of them, and that you shouldn't be treated like the beasts that had thick hides to keep out the cold on a howling winter's night. But you was only a cottar loon, and of no great consequence to anyone in particular, except your own mother, and many a night she wondered how you fared in your damp bed, or if a rat had chewed another hole in one of your socks.

The only other pieces of furnishing in your chaumer at Knowies was a chair and your own kist, but as you was never likely to have more than one visitor at a time, and mostly a neighbour loon as lonely and miserable and ill-used as yourself, there was never any scarcity of seats. Most lads just sat on their kists anyway, and you could easily play a melodion or a fiddle sitting on your kist, or take a bit blow at the mouth-organ, if you had an inclination for such things, or you could lie on your bed and read a book, waiting for your mind to take a turn in the direction you was supposed to go.

The lads before your time at Knowie's had their names burnt out with a hot poker on the walls and around the fire-place, and you could see by the list that the place had been well tenanted. Some of them had started on the floor, even on the seat of your only chair, but you resisted the temptation to add

46

even your initials to this conglomeration of immortality.

The door of Knowie's chaumer was at the back, or rather it had two doors, one on the inside and an outer door on the porch overlooking the sharn midden. This porch was like a prison observatory, and the likeness was strengthened by the long flight of stone steps and the iron hand-rail leading down to the cobblestones and the cartshed pends.

The stink of the sharn midden would be with you all the time, which made you glad of the skylight at the end of your bed, for by standing on the chair you could open the skylight and gaze out over the farmhouse and the garden, which were completely separate from the steading. On a fine day you could see Knowie's dothers on the bleaching green, where they would be hanging out Knowie's long drawers on the clothes line, and maybe some other bits of things you wasn't supposed to see, and but for this you might have given them a whistle through your fingers. Faith but you like the twa quines, Sadie and Nora, even though they were a bit older than you. Sadie the eldest was blonde and friendly but the Nora quine was the one that you fancied, her with hair as black and soft as nightfall and a bonnie sparkle in her eyes, and you would have liked fine to be her lad, but you feared that if Knowie got wind of such a thing he would most likely put you in your place.

Knowie was mostly seated at his parlour window, reading his newspaper, and the moment you saw him fold it up and take off his glasses you knew he would be over to the stable with the working orders for the afternoon. Always on the dot Knowie was, and you could set your watch on the minute he folded his newspaper, or your alarm clock from the moment he rapped on your chaumer door for the morning milking.

Knowie was a great lad for "The Times" newspaper. Him bein' with the gentry he had to have a newspaper different from the other fairmer lads, who said he sometimes talked over their heads, him bein' educated, like.

But by all standards Knowie was a good farmer. He kept his place tidy and worked the land in season. Over the years he had built up a fine herd of Friesian cows, with two or three of the Jersey breed to raise a cream on his milk. He was far ahead of

his neighbours for miles around, for while they were content
to poke about in the dark with paraffin lanterns he had his
place all lit up with electricity from storage batteries,
generated by his own dynamo and diesel engine.

There was even a light high up on a pole above the steading to
let you see over the midden with a barrow of dung in the dark.
Knowie switched it on first thing in the morning, when he came
to chap on your chaumer door, so you might have thought it
was for fear you fell down the stone steps and broke your neck;
but damn the fears, for it was to let his neighbours see that
Knowie was up and about on the stroke of five. For there was
nae sleepin'-in at Knowie's, and the chiel fair prided himsel' in
the fact that his customers never had to wait for their milk.

And if the neighbours were up b'times they would rub their
bleary eyes and stare at this new star in the mirk. But Dod
damned when daylight came and the star was sometimes still
in the sky they saw it was just one of Knowie's ferlies and
they wondered what the hell the chiel would try next.

They didn't have long to wait, for what does the chiel do but
off to the toon and comes back with a tractor, a blue Fordson
thing with spade-lug wheels on a motor-lorry. Och it was only an
iron-wheeled tractor and it couldn't go much on the road, so the
billies round about took a bit lauch at Knowie ahin his back and
said it was just another of his daft ploys. Some of them said it
would even raise his account with Old Brookie the blacksmith,
'cause young Knowie yonder would soon have everything
broken with a beast like that about the place.

But it was a different story when the Spring came; when the
grun was fair ettlin to be harrowed, hungry for seed, and his
neighbours horses dyin' of grass-sickness, for Knowie's tractor
was careerin' over the drying furrows with a set of iron-toothed
harrows dancing behind it, and a clamour of white gulls squacking
for grub.

And Knowie got a new drill-sower, with the smell of fresh
paint still about it, and though it was a narrow thing compared
with broadcast sowing it saved him a lot of harrowing-in; so he
had his crops all sown and his grass-seed in before the other
lads had barely started, and they shook their heads sadly and

said the man would soon be growing two crops in one season. And on a quiet morning you could hear the rattle of Knowie's metal rollers away up on the Stonehill, three of them coupled to the tractor thing and raising a cloud of dust, and the lads said he would raise the very devil from his foundry.

But there were some who were envious and even jealous of Knowie and his go-ahead ways, especially with that midden licht shining every morning, and one carle took it so much to heart that he played a prank on Knowie. And what does this carlin do but gets up in the dead of darkest night and opens the sluice at the Knowhead and drains all the water out of the dam. Not once but several times the wretch did this, and Knowie couldna get a thrash, because there was no water to drive his mill-wheel, and when his barn was empty he was in a sore stramash.

Say what you like about Knowie, but he didn't get the polis. The crafty chiel had an answer for this, so away he goes to the millwright and comes back with a length of belting on the milk lorry. Now this tractor thing had a pulley on it, like a traction-engine, so he whirrs it round and into his barn, couples up the belt with a pulley sic-like on the mill and he had the thing bummin' in no time at all.

Dyod but the folks thocht he had fair gone clean skite and this tractor thing was sure to set fire to his barn. But it fair garred the mull dirl or it was nearly riven off its trestles and the dust was comin' oot at the skylights. Out by in the sunhaze you could hear Knowie's mill snarling at the sheaves and abody slavin' wi' their sarks aff and spittin' stuff like tar.

Daggit now if Knowie doesn't go and gets the millwrights out of the town to put wheels on his threshing mill, and drags it out of the barn with the tractor, over to the stackyard for a thrash. So there was no fear now of Knowie having a fire in his barn, though yon coorse tyke that drained his dam maybe had a mind to go in the night and set fire to it himsel'.

Och, but the chiel will never get a thrash on a windy day: athing will be blawn' awa', and it will take a hantle of corn to pay for that contraption. Well now, if he doesn't go and gets a trusser thing fixed on to the tail of his mill and not a straw

49

is lost. Havers man! and he gets a wind-blast for the chaff, a long tube that blows the stuff up in the air and the billies out by couldna see what he was doing for the sture.

And it fair maddened them! Had the man gone clean wud? The orra slipe! Ah well, there was one consolation: he would find it damned expensive to pay for the binder-twine for that trusser thing. Surely it was enough to bind the stuff in hairst withoot a second time, and serve 'im right if 'es key tak' obstruction eatin' the tow among their straw.

Och-on-noo Skirlie! What's this ye tell me? Knowie wi' a motor car! Profits winna hide man. That melk's fairly payin' but the folk in the toon says he is a bittie scrimp wi' the measure joog. But that's whaur the car has come from! Of coorse we kent he had a motor for deliverin' his melk; ye canna grudge the man a motor for his melk when Cairnie and the Mulltoon has wan — but a motor car for pleeshure — Gweed preserve a' livin' soul!

But thon quines will be a hud doon tae Knowie yet! You mark my words Birkie, they'll be a pair o' randies among the lads yet. The Vricht was tellin' me yon Nora quine's havin' a gie carry on wi' that coonter-loupin' lad from the Howe Shop. I dinna ken what Knowie will say when he kens that his dother is taking up her time wi' yon white-faced scrat o' a crater, and him hardly got a brown copper to clap on anither — a' gone on drink.

Ah weel Skirlie, Knowie will likely be the last one to hear aboot that; but when he does most likely he'll go into a sulk; it's the nature o' the chiel, but a glaiket breet when he's got a dram in, which isn't often, him bein' parsimonious, like; though yon wife o' his is maybe at the back o' that, and her all dolled up to the nines in a fur coat and as much poother on her face as would bake a scone.

Aye Birkie, and they tell me she has gotten an electric iron for Knowie's Sunday sark, him bein' an elder o' the kirk, like, and needing' a clean sark every Sunday. Ach, but a good old-fashioned box-iron does fine wi' my gweedwife, a body canna afford a' that trock. But they will a' cost Knowie a bonnie penny yet. Fegs aye, they're juist gaun some far alength wi' their pride!

Dyod aye Skirlie, and yon loon, young Knowie yonder; they say he's fair terrified o' his auld man, fleein' up and doon the neep dreels in his sark tails, clean gaen gite, and his horse in a foam o' sweat, tryin' to raise dreels and the grun nae half made wi' yon tractor thing; nae even grubbit, juist scrattet on the tap wi' yon disc things. Did 'er ye hear the like o' that? And his mither oot after him with tea and fancy biscuits on a tray to try and simmer 'im doon. The fee-ed laddie was drivin' oot muck in the dreels and he said it was the only time he had ever gotten a drop tea syn he gaed to the place.

And Knowie's wife laid off about how they wouldn't get a cup of tea from the twa quines; "twa spoiled bitches," she called them, and that they didna ken what it was to do a day's work, or what it was to be hungry. And then she tells the loon to hurry up and drink their tea afore Aleck's father comes home with the melk cairt, 'cause he doesna take a piece himsel' in workin' hours and he doesna like to see ither folk at it.

Fie man Birkie, but the coneit o' some folk is most extraordinar! But young Knowie yonder could maybe go to the drink yet and land in the herbour; the wye he flees aboot in his father's car ye wad think he hadna another minute to live!

Losh aye Skirlie, but they have the telephone now up at the Knowehead, and Knowie's wife has a talk with the minister's wife or the dominie any hour of the day, making arrangements for the kirk social or the bairns concert, and they were sayin' at the Rural that the gentry are fair deaved wi' Knowie's wife since they got the telephone.

Aye Birkie, but a body might be glad o' Knowie's telephone and I think it's a grand thing for the farmin' folk, especially if ye had to get the vet or the houdi in a hurry; it might save ye sendin' for the knackery cairt or the hearse in the lang run, nae tae compare beast wi' body like, but it canna be helped.

But mair than that, for Knowie was tellin' yon lad up in the Reisk (yon futret o' a crater that kens athing) Knowie was tellin' him (or so he says — if ye can believe it) that they have the wireless now at the Knowhead. Nae one o' they crystal sets with the halter on't for yer lugs — na faith ye, something better than that for Knowie! He calls it "a loud-speaker radio," a varnished cabinet thing, with a bit horn on it, like a gramophone, and Knowie gets the time o' day from yon mannie away in London yonder, 'cause ye know how particular Knowie is about the time o' day. But fancy that mannie speakin' to Knowie in his parlour all the way from London, and telling him all about the weather a two three days in front, and Knowie knows when to sow his corn or ploo his neep park afore the weather breaks. Forewarned is forearmed, as Knowie says, him bein' educated, like.

Aye Skirlie, but he'll be the speak o' the Reisk noo if yon claik o' a crater has got hold on't. But I will say this for Knowie, that durin' yon big snawstorm last winter he saw that the toonsfolk got their melk. He had Aleck rigged out wi' his pair in a snawploo and he made a sledge and loaded it wi' cans and followed Aleck wi' the orra beast.

Yea man, but speakin' o' melk reminds me Birkie that ye dinna ken the verra latest, ye're a' ahin wi' the news man, for tae croon a' they've got the new melkin' machines at Knowie's noo — what say ye tae that? Yon quines are that bigsy and fear't tae fule their hands they wunna melk their father's kye, and Knowie has tae spend 'es money on a melkin' machine tae save the weemin folk. I'm damned if I'd lat a dother o' mine aff wi' that, I'd skelp 'er arse first. Dyod man, but the chiel will never melk a coo wi' yon thing, for a' the earth like a bloomin' octopus wi' its he'rt in its mou' — a mass o' rubber chubes that wad tie ye in knotts. It's like fower calves sookin' a coo and a' chawin' awa' at the same time. Nae beast will stand that. I tell ye man it's cruelty. Next thing ye'll hear they'll hae the Cruelty up at Knowie's, taraneezin' the beasts wi' yon things. And certain if ye leave they machines on yer coos owre lang ye'll draw bleed, and folk disna like bleedy melk, it' a fair scunner and he'll lose 'es customers in the toon. That'll be the doon come o' Knowie yet wi' his new-fangled wyes!

Ah well, Skirlie and Birkie had their say, and so had a lot more besides, but it just goes to show what happens when an energetic, enterprising man like Knowie tried to better himself just that little bit above his neighbours; but it was putting that midden licht above his steading that first set their tongues wagging.

But if you had been the fee-ed lad at Knowies you would have seen that some of the things they said were true, though not all of it. For one thing you wasn't hungered at the Knowehead, 'cause Knowie's wife fed you every day with a knife and fork, like you were with the gentry, and that was more than you could say about a lot of places you'd been at.

And you would be fillin' muck into a cart at the steading, on a cold morning with a brittle frost and icicles hanging from the spoots all round the roofs, and Knowie comes over the midden plank with a barrowful of cow dung, tips the sharn out of the barrow and then stands looking at you over the stilts. "Man," says he, "Ye've affa little go aboot ye sometimes. Ye're the first man I've seen fillin' muck wi' his jacket on!" Which was just another way of telling you to take it off! And not a very polite way at that, so you didn't do it. And you thinks that some day Knowie will maybe say that to the wrong lad, for you knew some lads who would have taken their jackets off right quick, but for a different reason, and maybe taught him a lesson. The impudence of the man. But ach, it wasn't worth risking your wages for, and he really wasn't such a bad stock once you got used to his high-mindedness.

But you didn't follow Knowie's destiny for longer than six months, for you were off when the term came, because of the hay-worms. You thought you would be high and mighty with Knowie and went and fee-ed to another place before he asked you to stay on, which he did, and was a real gentleman about it and had no bad feelings, and you was kind of mad at yourself for being so rash, especially when you were just beginning to get to know the quines better and all that.

And Knowie would shake hands with you when you left, which made you feel a real toff, and which was more than any farmer chiel would ever do with you again in your whole life, and his parting words would be: "Ye hinna been a bad ane!"

So that was Knowie, a most extraordinar man, as Skirlie and Birkie would say, and you would agree with them.

THE DOOKIT FAIRM

"An affa big dookit for juist twa doos!" That was the wye that
the folk outby spoke aboot the Dookit Fairm. Of coorse they
were referrin to the dwellin-hoose, a great big mansion amon the
trees, wi' as mony teem rooms as a beehive efter a swarmin, for
they had nae bairns at the Dookit Fairm. Elsie Wabster was
mistress at the Dookit, and she said she never would have a
littlin, and she never had a tooth pulled in her whole life, for
she said that raither than thole these tortures she wad dee.

The Dookit 'imsel was a queer mannie, and folk thocht that
this attitude o' Elsie's had something tae do with it, for there
seemed tae be something missin in the man's life, and though the
folk couldna fathom what it was they were sure it was the want
o' a bairn. And when he took a bit dander roon the sheep, wi'
the collie doggie at his heels, a body thocht it wad hae made a
great difference had it been a bit loonie hoiterin on ahin 'im.

But the maister o' the Dookit was most affa religious, though
nae exactly a Catholic, or he'd never hae put up wi' Elsie's
spinster wyes. But he was a staunch elder o' the Auld Kirk and
never said an ill-werd in his life, nae even in anger, and he had
the patience o' Job himsel in adversity. Strong drink never
touched his lips, nor pipe or fags, and his teachin o' the Sunday
School was a credit tae the presbytery.

Elsie was much the same, never missed a Sabbath at the kirk,
rain or shine, and the twa o' them wad set oot wi' the motor-
bike and side-car, and if it was rainin Elsie wad hoist her
umbrella tae keep aff the draps. And the Dookit wad squeeze

his horn "Pap-pap," tae put the bairns aff the road, and when
the bairns saw them comin they cried "here's Pap-pap!"

Noo the Dookit was a great lad for sheep, and he keepit
aboot three-hunder breedin yows wi' lambs at foot. And he
coontit 'es yowies in ilka park three times a day in the
simmer, fair terrified that a yowie should die on her back afore
the shearin. He could spot maggots on a sheepie's back nearly
a mile awa, and if he didna like the wye a lambie was waggin its
tail he was sure there was maggots on't, and mostly he was
richt. And juist gie 'im a yowie's hoof tae scrape at and ye
could hardly get 'im awa till 'es denner.

But Elsie wore the breeks, oh aye, ye could see that, 'cause
she was aye oot yappin at the back kitchie door when the grieve
cam roon tae see the Dookit aboot the wark. Elsie had tae
hae her speen in somewye, there was nae doot aboot that!

Noo the Dookit Fairm was a fairly big place as fairms go,
three-hunder-and-sixty-five acres arable, leased oot at a pound
an acre, which meant three-hunder-and-sixty-five pounds a
year, or a pound a day. So come what may, wind or weet, snaw
or sleet, every mornin that the Dookit rose and put on his
drawers he had tae mak a pound note clear profit afore the sun
set. And believe me, that was by no means easy in the days
that the Dookit was fairmin.

It gar't ye rub yer een in a mornin I tell ye, especially if
ye got a yowie lyin deid on 'er back, her legs sticking up like
spurtles and her een picket oot wi' the craws, 'cause that was
yer pound note nearly gone for a start. Ye could pluck the
wool aff the craiter afore ye buriet 'er (gin ye could stand the
smell) and maybe ye'd get a twa three shillins back for that
frae some rag tink.

And if a coo lost a calf, weel that was anither set-back. And
if ye got a horse or a mere lyin deid wi' grass-sickness that juist
aboot put ye oot at the door. Or maybe the neep-flea wad
ravage yer young plants afore ye got them hyowed, for there
was nae beetle-dust in those days. The craws could even clean
a neep park efter it was singled, lookin for the grub at the roots
o' the plants. Weel-a-wite, but sometimes ye was glaed o' the
craws, especially if ye saw them turnin ower the sods in yer lea

55

park, lookin for Leatherjackets, itherwise the Tory Worms wad leave yer corn crap as bald as an auld man's heid, and ye wad get a plague o' Daddy-lang-legs in the Autumn. But if the craws fell oot on yer tattie dreels that was a different story, and 'cause the Dookit never handled a gun in his life he was fair pestered wi' the black deils. They nestet thick in the trees a roon the big hoose and fair took advantage o' his hospitality.

And if the rings fell aff yer cairt wheels in a dry simmer ye couldna get yer peats hame; and if it was a weet simmer the rings bade on but yer peats wadna dry. Dyod man, ye've juist no idea o' the things that cam atween the Dookit and that pound note in the coorse o' a day.

But Elsie was his guidin star, as ye micht say, and what he couldna mak on the grun she wad save on the hoosehold expenses. Feed the men on what grows on the place, that was Elsie's motto: self-sufficiency, and but for a few triflin thingies, like saut, sugar and treacle, Elsie's scheme was verra nearly foolproof. Dyod aye, gin there had been troot in the mill-dam as there was hares in the parks Elsie had naething tae learn aboot feedin the five-thoosan.

Speak aboot a Shepherd's Calendar! Elsie had a menue tae beat a'. Ye could nearly tell what season o' the year it was by the food ye was eatin, and the days o' the week by yer diet. In the simmer when the eggs were cheap she preserved them, and ye ate them in the winter when they were dearer. That left mair fresh eggs tae sell at the richt time. Dyod aye, and when the butter wasna sellin she made saut butter, and ye got that and margarine when the price rose again. Sell butter and buy margarine, sound economics in those days when the price was sae much agley. And Elsie laid the table 'ersel, tae mak sure the men didna get ower muckle, a wee bittie o' butter aboot the size o' yer thoom-nail, a wee ballie or twa that wasna near aneuch; and the jam was the same, maistly rhubarb and wild raspberry, with strawberries for Sunday — a wee spoonfu that wad hardly stick a flea.

So ye got cabbage brose, kale brose, neep brose, melk brose and ordinar brose; melk broth and barley broth, leek soup, chappit tatties and skirlie or sise; stovies, hairy tatties (made

wi' hard fish and mustard sauce) peel-and-ate tatties and saut
herrin, oat-breid and skimmed melk — maistly onything
that grew on the fairm, plus peasemeal, and when ye mixed that
wi' oatmeal ye was still on hame grun.

And gin ye had a fancy for buttermelk ye could get that as
weel, or new-cheese when a coo calved. But Elsie never made
sowens; the miller kept his sids and his dist and ye was spared
the diet o' the Prodigal Son. But woe betide if ye got Elsie's
lintle soup made wi' margarine, for it wad fairly flatten ye,
and ye micht come tae yersel again aboot fower o'clock in the
efterneen, streekit oot on a grouth midden wi' a belly like a
bloatet yow.

But bein an auld bothy haun yersel ye didna mind a this
hame-grown whalesome fairin, nae gin Elsie had left the lambs
alane. But na faith ye! and gin a wee lambie died o' 'ooball in
the springtime Elsie had tae get it for the pot. Speak aboot the
Blood o' the Lamb! There wasna a drap o' bleed in the craiter's
body, and it was boiled white as a bleached dishcloth. And
teuch! Ye could hae chawed till ye was blin and never left a
teeth mark on't. But it saved a shillin or twa tae the butcher's
van and added that amount tae the Dookit's daily pound.

But a day was comin for Elsie folks said, or she wadna get
men tae bide at the Dookit. And come it did, but nae in a wye
that maist folk expectet. It's a wonder they said that they dinna
ate the rats at the Dookit, when they cam up in a plague oot
o' the mill-dam, and they swore that gin Elsie could get some
chiel tae shoot the rats and the craws she wad hae them on the
table. A rabbit or a hare was a richt at a time they said, but there
was no sayin how far Elsie wad go once she got startet....

But ye could aye tell when it was Sunday, 'cause ye got
porridge tae yer breakfast instead o' brose, and a fried preserved
egg instead o' a boiled ane. Ye was quite a gentleman on a
Sunday, and ye got a denner fit for a lord: stewed steak and
onions and chappit tatties, trifle for yer dessert, and even a
cuppie o' tea and a fancy piece. And all this was got ready on
the Saturday, because Sunday was a day o' rest and prayer for
Elsie, as it was for the Dookit 'imsel.
But there was nae pride wi' Elsie, that was wan thing; it

wasna pride that ailed 'er on a Sunday — it was her religion. But her sanctimony was a wee bit topsy-turvy, as ye micht say, 'cause ye fastet a' the week and on the Sabbath ye had the Feast o' the Passover. Maybe it should hae been the ither wye roon. But it was juist a sham wi' Elsie, and a good deal o' hypocracy, for nae sooner was Sunday by than ye was back tae the kale brose again, slubberin like swine.

And Elsie was sly too, for if a stranger cam in by, a mill-man or a lorry-driver, he got a stoup o' cream at his end o' the table, so that he wid cairry a good tale abroad aboot the mait at the Dookit. But fan Elsie gaed ben the hoose and ye showed the lad your joog o' separatet melk he was fair astonished and it thwarted Elsie's purpose. But there was wan thing that grew on the place that ye never tasted, and that was the honey. Na faith ye! for maist o' it gaed tae the Sale o' Work or ben the hoose.

Noo the Dookit had fee'ed a bit haflin tae ca' the fourth pair and sort a puckle nowt. He had tae haggle wi' the lad at the market 'cause the lad stak up for big siller. Twenty-three pounds for the sax months the lad had socht, from Whitsun tae Martimass, and the Dookit was only prepared tae gie twenty-one pound. But Elsie the jawd had telt 'im tae fee somebody respectable, and he liked the look o' the chiel, and Auld Keelie ower the dyke gaed 'im a gie gweed character, so the Dookit raxed anither pound. So the stock cam doon a pound and they had agreed for twenty-two pounds.

The chiel cam hame at the term on his bicycle and Elsie was waitin at the kitchie door tae welcome him intae his denner. She liked the looks o' the loon and maybe in a wye she wished she had ane sic like o' her ain. At yokin time the grieve had sent 'im back tae his last place wi' a horse and cairt for his kist, and the lad had settled doon fine wi' the other lads in the chaumer.

But the fourth pairie didna last lang, and gin the simmer was gaen they were pensioned aff on strae and watter and grew lang tails like colts. The blacksmith cam and took aff their sheen tae save expense and they gaed barfit like bairns and never felt kaim or brush on their hides again. Wi' corn at twal-and-saxpence a quarter it didna pey tae ploo, so the Dookit laid doon mair girse and gaed in for mair sheep. As for the nowt, man the chiel never saw a stirk yet, for the Dookit was that hard-up he couldna affoord tae buy them. Folk said that the fifty-odd steers he had in the byres were paid lodgers, belangin tae dealers and butchers wha paid for their keep, and of coorse the heid cattleman sortet them.

So the lad had a go at the sheep, lambin yows and sic like, pooed a pucklie neeps, howkit in the gairden, cleaned drains and ditches, mended a hen-coop or twa and helpit wi' the thrashin. Man, the chiel had that little tae dee that he got intae an affa easy-ozie kind o' wye, and he used to sit and sup his brose in the mornin wi' his spare haun in his pooch.

Losh aye, he wad never hae noticed it but the kitchie-deem tel't 'im aboot it when she cam in wi' her melk pails frae the byre.

"But lassie," says he, "I'm nae a bairn; I dinna need baith hauns tae haud ma speen. Gin it had been ham and eggs I was eatin, and usin a knife and fork, that wad be a different story. ..."

Of coorse he should hae been feenisht wi' his breakfast afore Jeannie cam in frae the byre, but syne he got rade o' his pair o' horse he didna hae tae rise sae early in the mornin as the ither lads, so he lay or the last meenit afore sax and was aye slubberin awa at his brose when the rest o' the lads were oot in the stable kaimin their horse. And sometimes the Dookit 'imsel cam ben the hoose and tied his pints at the kitchie fire, but the lad never turned a hair, juist gave the quine a bit wink if he caught her e'e when he left.

But this late risin gave the lad the only chance he had o' speakin tae the kitchie quine withoot the ither lads, and in nae time at a' they had taen a fancy tae each ither in secret. But the lassie was that hard ca'd in Elsie's service she hardly had time tae tak a bit maet, lat aleen look tae a lad. Fut wi' yarkin at yon lang-handled churn, melkin kye, feedin hens and swine, makin maet, bakin breid and scones, washin claes and dishes, cleanin firesides, cairryin peat and hackin sticks, makin up beds, scrubbin fleers, cleanin windaes and dustin ben the hoose, a'

that wark, the lassie was that tired or night she could hardly
rest in her bed. Frae five in the mornin till nearly ten at nicht
Jeannie was on her feet; frae cock craw tae owl hoot ye micht
say, and sometimes ironin a Sunday sark for the Dookit when
she should hae been anaeth the blankets. Elsie fairly held 'er
at it, shakin basses and ae thing or anither, and never a nicht
aff withoot a thraw, and only half-a-Sunday ance a fortnicht
efter kirk time, nae time at a' tae look tae a lad.

So the chiel was hert sorry for the quine, for he liked her
fine, and maybe in a year or twa he'd set up hoose o' his ain
and mairry her. It wadna be much o' a hoose, juist a bit
but-and-ben she could tak some interest in and hae mair
time tae 'ersell. But gie Elsie her due she saw the wye the
wind was blawin and took an interest in the pair o' them. She
couldna dee't 'ersel but she got the Dookit tae melk the kye
every second Sunday nicht tae gie the lassie a langer day aff, and
she tel't the chiel he could sit langer at the kitchie fire at
nichts than the ithers, him and the quine, and she saw that the
lassie got a nicht aff ance a week. So under Elsie's smilin pro-
tection this love affair grew, and in her ain religious wye she
felt she was doin the richt thing by the young couple. She
mithered the quine and upbraided the chiel until she had them
eatin oot o' her haun so tae speak, and a stranger body wad hae
thocht they waur her ain bairns.

The Dookit 'imsel was fair astonished at Elsie's interest in the
lad he'd fee'ed and the servant quine, and something o' her ain
youth seemed tae return in the process. She becam a different
woman athigither and less interferin in the wyes o' the place.
She began tae tak mair interest in the hoose than she did in the
fairm, and she had been mair o' a wife tae the Dookit in these
last months than she had been in years before. Even the man
'imsel felt a change in his ootlook though nae withoot a little
annoyance that the young couple should claim sae much o' his
wife's attention, though he was pleased and gratefu that his
wife should seem sae happy and pleased wi' hersel in a wye he
had never seen 'er afore.

And it didna seem tae maitter tae Elsie noo whaur the Dookit
got his daily pound and she fed the men like lords. Folk couldna

60

believe the change in the woman was natural, and they shook
their heids sadly for the day when she wad be locked up, clean
gaen gite. And a' withoot the Lord's blessin, for ye never see her
at the kirk nooadays, and the Dookit sits in a pew 'imsel like
an oolit in a sauch tree. And the wye she sottered ower that
young pair at the Dookit was the clipe o' the parish, and they
were only the bairns o' cottar folk, that were thocht tae be
below a woman o' Elsie's standin. It was an evil thing she did
folk said amon themsels: a loon and quine o' that age dinna
need encouragement; but the Lord will be avenged they said,
and he will send a plague upon Elsie at the Dookit, you wait
and see. ...

So the Lord sent a great plague upon Elsie as they had said,
and a great swarm o' rats came up oot o' the mill-dam and
overran the Dookit fairm. They were runnin thick in the close,
muckle scabby deils that were as tame ye could kick them
against the wa's, and the verra strae in the barn was a hobble
wi' rats. The Dookit wadna lay pooshin for fear o' killin the
hens. He set traps and cages and took a few, and when the cages
were full he got the new lad tae dip them in the dam tae droon
the squirmin brutes.

But Elsie had a better idea, so she took a duster and polished
the Dookit's silver-mounted double-barrelled gun that stood in
the hall beside the grandfather-clock and gave it to the chiel.
The Dookit had never fired a shot wi' it in his life; it had
belonged to his father but the Dookit had always been too tender-
hertet tae use it. He hated killin in a' its forms and wadna tramp
on a worm or a beetle gin he could help it. But he jumped on his
motor-bike and went to the emporium for a big box o' cartridges
for the chiel tae rid the place o' rottans, for surely that was no
evil the Dookit thocht.

So the chiel took the gun and hid 'imsel in odd corners roon
the steadin and the big hoose and baitet the rodents wi' bruised
corn. When about a dizzen rats had gaithered roon the bait the
lad let fly wi' baith barrels and blew them tae smithereens. And
the chiel was weel content wi' this amusement, 'cause efter the
evenin's shootin he was treatit in the hoose wi' tae and fancy
pieces and he could while awa the time wi' his lass.

At nicht when the licht was gettin dim the chiel baitet the rats in the close and hid 'imsel in the hen-hoose. He was winnin this war on the rats and they were gettin scarcer and he sometimes had tae wait langer for a shoot. The rats were gettin wily as weel, and were sly at comin oot in the full licht o' day, so that only nightfall and hunger brocht them tae the bait.

It was gettin rael dark for Elsie had the lamps lichtit in the kitchie and ben the hoose. And when she had the tae ready she tel't the quine tae run and get her lad afore bedtime.

Noo the servant lass was a bittie feart at the clockin hens durin the day and she minded that she hadna gathered in a' the eggs. She wad look for her lad, but in the meantime she wad get the eggs. The hens wad a' be reistit and she could throw the clockers oot o' their nests and grab the eggs, for they wadna see tae pick 'er sae much in the gloom.

Noo the chiel was watchin 'es rats and juist aboot ready tae lat bleeze when his quine cam runnin owre the close. They began tae scatter, and juist when he fired baith barrels his lass bent doon tae enter the hen-hoose. Even as he pulled the triggers he saw her lurch owre his sichts; in the reek and smell o' poother he saw her fa'; even in the squak o' flyin hens ower his heid he heard her simper. The lad got sic a scare his hert nearly stoppit and he flang the gun on the fleer. His een were het wi' tears and he grabbed the quine in his oxter, her warm bleed on his face. He laid her doon canny, feart tae look gin she was deid, and ran for Elsie.

Elsie had heard the shot but thocht naething o't; she heard them ilka nicht, but when the chiel cam in soakin in bleed she got a sair fricht. "It's Jeannie," he grat, "I doot I've killed 'er!" And he sat doon on a chair and grat like a bairn. "Faur aboot laddie?" Elsie cried, shakin the chiel by the shooders, "faur's Jeannie?"

"In the hen-hoose!" And his voice rose frae his throat nearly like a scream.

Elsie cried on the Dookit frae ben the hoose and the pair o' them ran tae the hen hoose. But the lassie was deid and poorin wi' bleed, her face and breist shot tae tatters, so the Dookit jumped on his motor-bike and flew for the doctor. And when the doctor and the bobby cam they cairriet the lassie intae the fairm hoose and laid 'er on the fleer, and the loon sabbit and grat in Elsie's oxter as gin he had been a bairn.

Efter the funeral there was an inquest and a lot o' awkward questions speirt at the loon, though abody kent fine he had nae intentions o' shootin his lass. And Elsie was sair torn wi' guilt for gein the loon the gun that did it and she was hert sorry for the loon. She grat mony a day and priggit sair wi' the loon tae bide when the term cam roon. Tears were a thing that Elsie had never felt afore, unless they had been tears o' rage or jealousy, and the Dookit was sair perplexed at what could ail his wife.

The term day cam and the loon gaed doon the close for the last time. Elsie could thole her guilt nae langer and she ran doon the close efter the loon. She wad hae gi'en 'im the place tae bide on but it was hardly in her po'oer, but she grabbed the loon in her oxter and grat in his airms, and then the most affa thing happened tae Elsie, for she fainted in the close and the Dookit and the loon had tae cairry 'er back tae the fairm hoose.

So they got the doctor and he told the Dookit that his wife was in the family way, and the man could hardly control 'imsel. And neither could the neighbours: Michty me, Elsie wi' a bairn at thirty-echt, and anither doo in the Dookit; weel weel, that was what she got for encouragin that young pair aboot the place, though God knows, there was little need tae say mair aboot that; she wad hae her ain thochts aboot it nae doot.

THE BEGGAR LAIRD
A Legendary Fragment from Buchan History

Lachbeg House, that fairyland palace in the depths of the woods.
The sun scarcely reached the avenues in summer because the
trees were so dense. And the lovely lake, dark and smooth as
glass, where the luxuriant rhododendrons, mauve, purple and
white, were reflected on the surface. Swans white and graceful
glided around the satin-green islands, arching their long necks to
dip their heads in the water. The waterlilies were just out of
reach, where they floated in islands of yellow wonderment.
Irises protruded their crimson tongues in mockery of our in-
ability even to touch them. Willows dipped their green feathery
tresses in the water, while laburnum spangled the banks with
its gold. There were two rustic arbours on the banks of the lake,
where you could sit and watch the water-hens jerking in and out
among their nests in the reeds. There was also a boathouse with
a flat-bottomed cobble tied up inside. The wood paths were
veined with tree roots where the feet of many travellers had
exposed them.

Sometimes on a Sunday, with my cousins Selby and Teddy
Joss, we used to sneak away from our grandfather's farm to spy
on the laird's palace. Gleg Handerson was my grandfather's
name, and he said that if the head gamekeeper saw us on the
laird's policies he would shoot us. And besides, there were signs
marked PRIVATE all over the place. But we wouldn't be
deterred. Fascination overcame fear and we dared every risk to
satisfy our curiousity.

A huge mastiff sat at the front door. Folks had heard the

factor say he would tear a man to pieces. But we knew better, or thought we did, because we went to school with the head gardener's bairns, and they said that if you went close enough he would lick your face. He was only an ornament they said, and that he could hardly be bothered to scratch the flies from his own ears.

Maybe the factor was only trying to scare us off? It was awfully tempting to try and see who was telling the truth. The trouble was we never got near enough to find out. We were too scared. The great house was so forbidding, and the air of wonderment so entrancing we could only lie in the long grass and watch at a distance.

When we reached the clearing in the woods Lachbeg House was a wonderful sight. It almost took our breath away every time we saw it. It made us gasp with excitement. We just lay down eager to watch, thankful that the gamekeeper hadn't seen us after all.

There it stook on its green, carpet-smooth terraces, high and white and wonderful. The sunlight was trapped in the clearing and shone on the walls like a spotlight. Far out at sea sailors could see those bartizan turrets above the trees in Lachbeg Woods, just as they could see the white stone deer on the Mattock Hill, when the weather was clear.

Folks said there were as many doors and windows in Lachbeg House as there were days in the year, and dungeons deep down in the earth where the old lairds kept their enemies prisoner in days long ago.

The modern part of the house stood in front, an Adams' Mansion, folks called it, pillared like a Grecian temple, with baskets of flowers hanging in the arcades. There were steps of marble up to the front entrance and a coat-of-arms above the massive door, varnished and studded with iron. A stone balustrade went round the roof, with a glass domed observatory in the middle, for looking at the stars. The chimneys were also on the roof, but squat and inconspicuous, so that you hardly noticed them. The towers and keep at the back were of an older date, much older, and looked like a fairy castle, with a flagpole high above the trees. Folk said that in the old days, when the laird was a young man, you would have seen a Union Jack flying from the pole. That was when the laird was home from abroad, and wearing his kilt of Fraser tartan, and to let his friends know they could come and visit him. But now the Laird had been at home for such a long time the flag was tattered to bits, and nobody had troubled to renew it. And besides, the laird didn't want visitors any more, he just wanted to sit and brood over his only son who had shot himself, and to listen to Gleg's pipes at twilight.

Twice a year our grandfather went to Lachbeg House to pay his rent. Folk said the laird was hard-up for siller and that the time would come when the tenants would get a chance to buy their farms; buy or move out for a higher bidder if you couldn't afford the price. But they said a sitting tenant would get the first option to buy his own holding privately. After all it was only fair after what some of them had spent on their places; the drains they had dug and the fences they had put up, the bits of heather they had taken in with the spade and the manure they had put on the land. "Fegs aye, it was but richt," Gleg had said. "It's but a hand tae mou' existence onywye!"

A day was set aside for the rent, and all the tenants got a high-tea and a dram — "Forbyes a bit keek at the hoosemaids," as Skirlie Wullie said.

The room where they paid the rent was awfully grand Gleg said: "Wi' great big picters o' the laird's ancestors glowerin' doon at ye, a table as lang as an endrig, and a carpet on the fleer as lush as a new-grass park. Man, the ceilin's like an iced-cake and I'll swear the chandileer wad weigh a hunderwecht. Lord aye, and a marble fireplace, as big as ye could coup a load o' peat in't." And while he told us this we sat at his feet wide-eyed and wonder-struck. And what about the mastiff? we asked. Weren't they afraid of the dog? Gleg said that he was tethered on rent days. Maybe, he promised, when we were men we would see this great room for ourselves; then we would see he had been telling the truth.

The laird sat at the head of the table in his kilt. Folk said he was almost imbecilic since his good lady died and that he took little heed of the proceedings. Nowadays the factor was boss.

66

"He has a face a' roon," said Skirlie, "like a took clock, and he fair thrives on't."

The factor put the money in a small black and gold band-box and the clerk signed the receipts. The tenants got a chance to lodge any complaints they had to make and the clerk wrote it down in a ledger for future reference. Long Tom Stag might be needin' drain pipes for thon weet howe o' his, or Hardyards might be needin' the roof of his barn repaired, or a new cement floor in his kitchen. Maybe the travises in Cairnie's coo byre needed replacement, and there was a demand for paint, slates, bricks, new doors and windows and sic like. That wasn't saying that everybody got what he wanted. Not unless he asked often enough. And sometimes a body got tired o' askin' and just paid for the damned thing himsel'. "Ach weel," as Jeely Pom would say: "The fairm will maybe be yer ain someday onywye. Sae lang as ye dinna big a new neep-shed, or a dung-coort, 'cause that wad put up the price o' yer ain fairm when it cam' tae buyin' it." And the rest of the billies cried "here here!" and said that Jeely Pom's heid was fairly screwed on the right way and that all his back teeth were up.

A lease was based on a cropping rotation system which was considered fair to proprietor and farmer. It lasted for fourteen years but a tenant had a break in seven. He could move out if he wasn't satisfied. On the other hand, at the end of seven years, if the laird had a grudge against a tenant (if the tenant was neglecting his land for instance — or fell in arrears with his rent) the laird could refuse to renew his lease. But to show how seldom this happened you only had to go to the old graveyard beside the Parish Kirk at Lachbeg, where you could see that most of Lachbeg's tenants had been born on their farms, and that generations for more than a hundred years back had their names carved on the old leaning gravestones. Indeed these gravestones were a sort of guarantee that you couldn't be far wrong to rent a farm on the Lachbeg estate.

Folk said it would be a sorry day for the tenants when the old laird should die. The estate would go to his daughters, they said, and they were high and mighty, and would put up the rents and wouldn't repair the steadings.

We hadn't seen any of the laird's three daughters, but folks who had said their faces were painted and powdered like they weren't real, and delicate as a butterfly's wings, that wouldn't stand a shower o' rain or a nip of frost, and that their hair was dyed and their fingernails varnished, and that it would take a year's rent from the tenantry to pay for the gaudy dresses they wore. That was gentry for you, and folk said they couldn't stand our winters anyway; that they went away to sunny lands at the first hint of snow and didn't come back until the swallows returned. So what could you make of that when your wife hadn't been out of the close for a six-month and you yourself had never been further than the marts in the toon.

Meantime we could see the great dog lying on his paws at the top of the marble steps, like a lion on guard over his master. We daren't make a sound lest he prick his ears. He knew we were there. He could smell us. We knew by the way he turned his big snout and sniffed the air in our direction, but it seemed he just couldn't be bothered to come and look for us. Maybe it was true what the bairns said about this dog: that he was just an ornament; but none of us would dare to stand up and challenge him, we just lay there watching, listening, whispering. ...

Sometimes through the ferns we could see a coach at the front entrance; a grand coach with four white horses, and it was all so Cinderella — like we really thought we were in fairyland. The fact is that the laird wouldn't hear of a motor car and still kept a coach and driver for his daughters and business trans-actions.

But there was something else about this wonderful place that reminded us of Cinderella. We all knew the story of the Beggar Laird, who had been one of the present laird's ancestors. One night long ago, as this laird lay in his richly curtained bed in Lachbeg House, he had a strange dream of a lovely girl he knew who lived in Rockbulge Castle, about twelve miles ride away, on the seashore. This young lady was an orphan who lived with her aunt and uncle who were her guardians and trustees of the castle and estates until she came of age to look after them herself. And the laird dreamed that her aunt and uncle were trying to poison the heiress with a goblet of wine, so that they could inherit the lands of Rockbulge.

He saw the maiden in her bed, a finely carved four-poster, while her aunt leaned over her with the glass of poisoned wine. She held the goblet in her lace-frilled hand, and each time she proferred it the maiden pushed it away, while her uncle stood by in his shirt-sleeves, anxious and scowling. They were about to man-handle the girl and force her to swallow the wine when the laird woke up.

He tried to sleep again but found he couldn't. Each time he closed his eyes the same graphic picture came before him. The realism of his dream stung him into action, so he arose and attired himself as a tramp, saddled his horse and rode full tilt to Rockbulge Castle.

It was a clear night, with the moon dipping from one fleecy cloud to the next, and the wind whistled in his ears. When he reached Rockbulge, high on the cliff-tops, the moon glittered on the sea and the waves boomed against the rocks. There was only one approach to the castle, across a narrow ledge of rock, and if this was guarded he would have to swim the ravine. Meanwhile he hid in the woods and tethered his horse to a tree. He smeared his face with earth, cut himself a staff and hobbled towards the ridge. But there was no one there, so he scrambled across and made for the castle. He rapped on the heavily studded door to summon the guard. When the door creaked open on its rusty hinges the guard looked at him with a spluttering torch held high above his head. Our laird said he was a soothsayer and wanted but a night's shelter in the castle for his aching bones. If they would only give him the warmth of the kitchen faggots it would ease his aches and pains he said, since he had journeyed far, and in return he would read the good lady's fortune on the morrow.

"I come in peace," he said, "I carry no sword, nor have I any knife in my doublet. I can do no harm to your household. But I have travelled far; I am weary and footsore, if you will but give me peace to lie down I shall be thankful."

Now folks were superstitious in those days and loth to turn away a palmister. Perhaps if you turned them away they might leave a curse on your doorstep, and the household might fall on evil times. He looked harmless enough to the guard as he held the torch higher to look at the tramp; a mumbling old fool with tattered clothes, a crooked back and leaning on a stick — He had a good mind to kick him over the precipice. But the tramp had thought of this as well, and with a keen eye he watched the guard from under his hood — just waiting for him to try it.

So the guard admitted the soothsayer, and very soon he pretended to be fast asleep on a rug by the kitchen fire. Several of the guards came and took a look at him, but satisfied that he was harmless they soon retired to the keep. But the laird was soon on his feet, alert as a deer, and by the light of the fire he crept towards the castle door, where he slipped the bar from its sockets to assist his escape.

His shoes were wrapped in sackcloth and he made no noise. He crept up the great staircase to the bedchambers, high up in the castle, and along the dark corridors, quiet as a cat, until he saw a light under a door; the maiden's door he was sure, for he had been in the castle before and knew it well.

The young laird listened at the door, his heart beating in his ears, but he could hear nothing. But the urgency of his dream was still upon him and he felt he must act quickly. He lifted the hasp gently, noiselessly, and the door opened, and as it widened his dream came alive in the candlelight.

There on the high-posted bed was the maiden, distressed and in tears, and almost convinced by her aunt that she was sick. Over her stood her aunt with the goblet of wine, and by her side was her man in his shirt-sleeves. The girl's hands were reaching out in a tremble for the goblet when the laird shattered the scene. He had caught them in the very act of murder.

But the laird was lightning quick. He dashed the cup from the woman's hand and gave the man a crack on the jaw that bewildered him. The woman attempted to scream but the laird held his hand over her mouth. She bit savagely at his fingers, but with his free hand he ripped a tassled cord from the bed and wrapped it round her body, lacing her hands to her sides. He was about to stick the tassle in her mouth when she fainted in his arms, so he threw her on the bed. Her man revived and rose unsteadily but the laird chopped him down again. An open-hander on the side of the neck crumpled him into a heap.

The maiden was even more surprised but the laird gave her
no time to ask questions. "Wrap yourself in a blanket," he said,
"and come with me."

He seized her hand and dragged her from the bed, picked her
up and carried her down the stairs, out into the cold night
towards the ridge. How she got across there in her nightdress she
could never recall. It was like a nightmare, with the laird holding
her hand and guiding her bare feet on the hard stone, while on
either side the chasm yawned and the water splashed and gurgled
in the darkness. Once across this obstacle they made for the
woods, where the laird untied his horse and set her on the
saddle. He gathered the reins and sprang up behind her. Next
moment they were off, her hair in his face, streaking through
the fading moonlight. The laird dug his heels into his horse's
ribs and rode hard for Lachbeg.

Once in the shelter of Lachbeg Woods he felt they were safe
from pursuit. He stopped his horse and slid the lady to the
ground. "Wait here," he said, "by this tree, and I'll be back
for ye." For he didn't want her to think that the laird of
Lachbeg had hired a tramp to rescue her. He would carry her
home in the style that she deserved, worthy of her breeding.
So he galloped off into the wood, while the maid waited in her
blanket, her teeth chattering in the cold. It was lithe here in
the sighing woods but she shivered a little in the darkness.

She wondered why the tramp had left her here so helpless,
unless it were to fetch his master, and he was such a long time
about it he must have forgotten her. But lo, he was back at last,
the young laird in all his finery, and he threw a warm cloak
about her shoulders. Morning light was breaking through the
woods and when the maiden saw this braw knight before her
she would have nothing to do with him. The laird thought
she must be joking. But no, she was dead serious. No wonder
he had deceived the guard in his errand of mercy.

"Your aunt was trying to poison you," he said, "You must
never go back to Rockbulge."

"I believe you, fair cousin," said the heirress, "but where is
the beggar man who rescued me?"

71

"Fair damsel," said the laird, "believe me, I am the beggar man. I had a dream that you were in danger and I was just in time to spare your life."

"Your dream may be true, fair sir. Indeed I do not doubt it, since your worthy servant arrived so opportunely. But why didn't you rescue me yourself? Show me the poor beggar man who risked his life to save me. I will share my life with him, rather than be your lady."

"But you are being childish," the laird protested, "believe me, fair lady, I am the beggar man."

But the maid was adamant. "Show me the beggar man," she insisted; "let him speak for himself. I will not go on your horse until this is so."

So the laird left her again by the Eildon tree and rode back to Lachbeg House. He took off all his finery and dressed himself in rags, even to smearing his face with earth as he had done before.

He laughed to himself as he rode back to the maiden, and she smiled also when she saw him. When he dismounted he threw her arms about his neck and kissed him. "I believe you, my lord," she said, "you are indeed my beggar man." So he picked her up and set her on his horse and led her home to be his lady.

They lived happily for many years. Until about the middle of last century the Beggar Tree still stood in Lachbeg Woods. The tree where the lady waited for the laird to return a beggar. During the whole of her life this lady gave orders that food was to be left in a cleft of this tree for passing beggars. And all the days of her life the soothsayers blessed her, and muttered her name in all their prayers, and she had a life of great happiness and raised a family that were the pride of Scotland.

Her husband was beloved by all. Eventually Rockbulge came to his estate but his lady sold it again. She said she had no memories of that old castle; that her life didn't begin until she came to Lachbeg. With the money the two of them made vast improvements on the estate; planting trees, building dykes, draining, housing the poor, and although they didn't leave this lovely mansion house as we were looking at it now, at least they gave us the castle behind it. Since the days of the Beggar Laird and his fair lady no man had ever had to lift his bonnet to Lachbeg, not even a tink with his besoms, for they had left a latin inscription on the family insignia which read: "All men are equal," and for many generations the sons of Lachbeg had honoured it.

But now the spell was broken. The shot that dealt the laird's son his self-inflicted wound had shattered it. The old laird was now a dottard and his inheritance was uncertain.

And now the mastiff gave a bark and shook me out of my daydreams. It sent us scurrying back to the wood like frightened rabbits. But now he was on the lawn, bounding towards us with an arched back, the turf flying from his paws. In a moment he was upon us, all three in a heap, rolling over and over, licking our faces in a great frolic. Before long we were sticking our small fists into his great mouth, while he stood gasping with his tongue out and laughing at us with his eyes.

But we were only boys. It was easy to play with us now. But is there not some great Greek philosopher who once said that what a man loves most he must finally destroy. And it made my heart sad to think that someday we might come back as men, with picks and drills and sticks of dynamite, to savage and destroy the glory of this great house.

In reaching for the stars man is destroying his earthly heritage. He must tax the one to finance the other, and thus these iconoclastic tendencies have become fashionable in our time.

Lachbeg House, my palace. Oh my fairyland. How my heart bleeds for thee.

MY UNCLE SIMON

It was sunny in the evening at Kelpieside. After supper old Gleg Handerson went outside to give his pipes a skirl at the kitchen gable.

There was something of the old Norsemen in my grandfather. You could see it in his blonde-grey hair, in the frown of his sand-coloured eyebrows; sometimes in his fierce, startled expression, when his steel blue eyes held you in a hypnotic stare.

There was something of the old Highlander in him too, for a dirk suited his leg well when he wore the kilt, and a sword would have been as a wand in his powerful grasp. He was passionate and morose, sullen and cheerful by turns, moods that long centuries of trampling the heather and tearing at the sod had bred in his ancestry.

You could hear the skirl of Gleg's pipes up on the Mattock Hill, where the Gaels in olden times had dug peat from its slopes. Folks long back had gathered huge white stones and set them in the shape of an antlered deer on the hillside. On a quiet evening you could hear the wail of Gleg's pibroch in the depths of Lachbeg woods, filled with all the sorrow of Flodden, of Culloden and Lucknow, and the laird would listen from his mansion, the crofter from his ingle, and all those who were heavy at heart found solace in the stricken music. Fingers that were clumsy and gnarled with work now took on a grace upon the chanter as they waltzed in ballerina charm upon the reeds that turned a man's breath to soul filled ecstasy.

But it wasn't every evening that Gleg played the pipes at the gable window. Even though it was sunny he would just sit on the old stone roller and stare at the ground. Then his brows would curl over his eyes and you could see the devil at work in his brain. He was as dour as the clouds that gathered on the Mattock Hill, and at any moment a glance from his eye would frizzle your soul like lightning.

Gleg was in one of his black moods and sat on his roller on the evening that my uncle Simon wanted to show me the oat-crusher at work. I think he wanted to show off a little of what he could do on one leg.

Uncle Simon had one of his legs sawn off in his closet when he was nine. His brothers and sisters heard the rasp of the doctor's saw on the bones. Sarah my grandmother ran back and forth between the peat fire and the closet with kettles of boiling water. And when it was all over the children saw the two doctors take Simon's leg away in a brown paper parcel, dripping blood to the doorstep. They said they even heard Simon screaming in the chloroform. Now Simon was a man and he felt his infirmity keenly.

The threshing mill and the oat-crusher were driven by water-power, by a long overhead cable that stretched from the water-wheel to a pulley outside the barn wall. The dam was a considerable distance from the barn and we had to walk past the farmhouse to reach it and open the sluice.

The oat-crusher made a fearful din and made the bells ring in my ears. Indeed I suspected Simon of trying to frighten me, so I stood in the barn to prove he was wrong, and I was just about the age when Simon got his leg off.

After the oat-crushing, when we were on our way back from closing the dam sluice, old Gleg was on his roller putting straw in his boots. We were almost abreast of him when his mood snapped. He stood up from the roller with one of the heavy tackety boots in his hand.

"Simon," says he, "wha said we was needin' corn bruised?"

"Oh naebody," Simon whined, "I juist thocht when there was plenty watter in the dam we should tak' the good o't."

"Ye wad run the place yersell eh? Ye think ye're maister here nooadays and I'm naebody, eh? Efter this ye'll wait till ye're tell't tae dae a job, d'ye hear?"

Simon sensed a threat and said nothing, but moved off in the direction of the barn, his wooden leg creaking at every step.

Gleg stood for a moment, watching him, the boot in his hand, held by the tab at the back. Simon ignored him and Gleg took it as a challenge to his authority. He raised the iron-studded boot high over his head and sent it hurtling into the air in Simon's direction.

His aim was sure and direct, and the iron heel of the boot struck the retreating Simon smack on the back of the head. He reeled and staggered against the cart-shed pillar and raised his hands to his ears as if he had been struck deaf.

The hens in the close got such a fright they were flying in all directions. The pigeons flapped up from the ground and alighted on the coping of the red-tiled barn. Sarah, my grandmother came out from the cow byre with a pail of milk in each hand. When she saw her son staggering in the close she dropped her pails and ran to support him. "Oh Simon," she cried, "what has come over ye?" She spilled the milk in the close and the turkey-cock gobbled in alarm as he ran out of her way.

My aunts Nora and Kirsty came out of the kitchen, my cousin Selby behind them, and they all ran towards Simon, who still stood with his hands over his head by the cart-shed wall. He took away his hands and there was blood on his fingers. They all stared at him and all of them questioned him at the same time: "What has hurt ye Simon?"

Simon pointed a bloody finger at his father. "He threw a boot at me 'cause I opened the dam sluice withoot his orders!"

Gleg went hopping forward on one foot to get his boot back. When he picked it up he said: "Aye, and that'll learn ye that I'm still maister here; and if that doesna suit ye ye'd better clear oot and try yer luck somewhaur else on yer fung leg!"

"Think shame o' yersell," cried Sarah, shaking her fists at her husband; "shame on ye tae strike the crippled loon, efter a' he has gone through already." She went as near to Gleg as she dared and stamped her foot, like a ewe when a shepherd would take away her lamb, almost spat at him, like a cat.

"Ye've spoiled the devil," cried Gleg, pulling on his boot, "and he thinks he'll do what he likes about the place — but nae as lang as I'm maister here! Tak' 'im tae the hoose and gie 'im a sook!" And with that he turned away and went back to his roller.

A band of sympathisers circled Simon. They all moved over to the back kitchen door and squeezed inside amid a hubbub of voices.

The collie dog came out of his kennel, to the full length of his chain and began to yap at Gleg where he sat on his roller. Gleg let fly at him with a stone and he disappeared into the barrel with a yelp. When the pigeons thought it safe to descend they flopped down from the byre roof and strutted about the close among the hens, picking up what corn had been left in their absence.

Simon was not badly hurt, only a slight bruise and a smear of blood on the hair at the back of his head. But Sarah and his sisters made such a fuss over it that Simon made up his mind to take full advantage of their sympathies; to rally them all in his favour and have them all eating out of his hand and spitting on old Gleg till he came crawling back for forgiveness.

So Simon pretended to be worse than he was and said he would leave Kelpieside before dark. "Daw has ordered me frae the place," he whimpered, "and I'll go, this verra nicht!"

"But yer Daw didna really mean it Simon," Sarah remonstrated, "he was juist angered at the time and didna realise what he was sayin'."

"He meant it a' richt," Simon asserted, "and I wunna need anither tellin!"

Sarah began to weep and Nora tried to console her. Kirsty hung the kettle on the crook over the peat fire and set the tea-cups on the bare scrubbed table. It was getting dark inside so she lit the paraffin lamp that hung from the ceiling.

My uncle Jonas, who was Simon's younger brother, came into the kitchen and asked what was the trouble. He said he had spoken to Daw on his roller but had got no answer. Jonas had a croft of his own across the road and he only came in by to pass the time of day.

The tea was strong at Kelpieside, boiled in the brewing of it in a black enamelled tea-pot that never left the fireside.

"Heather Bree," folks called it, that came in by, and you got no milk in it, unless you went to the milkhouse yourself for a stoup of cream.

When tea was over Jonas and Simon lit their cigarettes from a cinder which Selby brought to them on the tongs from the peat ash. Then Simon went into his closet to bundle up his clothes for departure. There were more protests from the women but Simon was determined to bring their sympathy to full maturity, and turn them against old Gleg to his utmost.

Now he was ready to go and they all sallied out after him to the darkness.

Sarah looped her hand through Simon's arm and tried to pull him back. But he shook her off vigorously and limped boldly up the avenue. She implored him to stay, even to tears, and promised that all would be well with Daw. She would see to it she said. But Simon took no notice. Someone cried on Gleg, but he was gone from his roller, most likely in a sulk, and nowhere to be found.

Nora and Kirsty said goodbye to Simon at the head of the avenue. They were both in tears but nothing they could say would induce Simon to stay. But Sarah and Jonas wouldn't give up and I followed on behind them with cousin Selby. I felt partly guilty about the whole affair because Simon had wanted to show me the oat-crusher at work. Perhaps if I hadn't been here it might never have happened.

We were nearly a mile from home and Selby whispered to me that Simon must surely be in earnest; that he surely meant to go for good. But Sarah still clung to Simon and Jonas still reasoned with him.

But Simon wouldn't be dissuaded. He was a man now he said and wouldn't be talked to as if he was still a loon. And had not his father told him to clear out. Even though he was a cripple he wasn't going to submit to this sort of treatment.

Another quarter-of-a-mile and Simon stopped. He could go on no further and burst into tears. How he had managed thus far he didn't know. In his rush to get away he had forgotten his best friend. He didn't even know where he was going; or where he could spend the night. Anger and excitement had borne him along until now. But he could prevail no longer; not without his best friend on such a journey. Why hadn't he thought of it? His crutch!

Simon turned to Selby and asked him to run back for his crutch. Sarah wouldn't hear of it, for now she saw a chance to detain her crippled son. But even as they argued the wail of Gleg's pipes brought them to silence. It was faint but audible, every note as clear and distinct as a falling tear-drop — "Will Ye No Come Back Again?" was brought down on them with the soft evening breeze from Kelpieside; perhaps from the stackyard where Gleg would be piping round the rucks, his heart softened and the tears running down his face.

But Simon was ridiculed and heart-broken and sobbed out his grief in his mother's arms. So we half pushed half carried Simon back to the farm and shoved him into his closet.

Jonas unfastened the leather straps on Simon's shoulder and took off his wooden leg and set it in a corner. The stump was red and inflamed with the ordeal and Jonas tucked Simon in bed.

And Sarah took Simon's crutch and hid it for three days until he promised he would never leave home again.

AIKEY BRAE
A Great Many Romances Have Blossomed Forth on Aikey Brae And No Doubt They Still Do.

In the old days down in the How o' Buchan hoeing and haymaking were always associated with Aikey Fair. If you were finished with the hyow and well forrit with the hay you had a good chance of a day off for Aikey. The seasons were late in those days, because the working methods were more primitive, but if you had the hay in the "trump (trampled) cole" that was good enough, for there it could remain until the start o' hairst, maturing in the sun, when you could build it into rucks on dewy mornings, or when the weather was too damp for harvesting.

But of course the peats were another snag, and it was an awful punishment having to rickle peats on Aikey Day, when most other folks were away at the fair, so you did your damn-test to have the peats all set up on their ends to dry before Aikey. Aikey Fair was considered a general holiday, and apart from term and market days, and a day off at the New Year, it was about the only holiday you would get.

Wednesday was the recognised day of the Fair, the first Wednesday after the nineteenth of July, but if your boss wasn't a kirk elder you could jump on your bike and take a run up on the Sunday before then, when the fun really started, and if you didn't care a damn you went in any case, but sometimes it was frowned upon in those days.

Aikey used to be a horse-fair, when all the lads would be there with their horses for the market, their manes rolled and their tails tied up with coloured segs, standing in rows like patient cavalry, waiting a buyer. They must have missed a lot of the fun these lads, standing all day with a horse on a lead; sometimes without a bite of dinner, unless the dealer gave them a tip, and the cottar lads spent most of it on a sweetie for the bairns.

But that there was fun at Aikey in those days there is no doubt; even though you didn't have much to spend, your money went a long way compared with nowadays. For one thing a bicycle was cheaper to park than a car, and if you wanted to save a sixpence on that you could throw your bike into a hedge at Old Deer and walk up the hill for nothing. There used to be acres of bicycles parked at Aikey, and "Old Briggie", the farmer of Bridge-end said it was the best paying field he had, though he never planted anything in it but bicycles, and that but once a year, while it lay in grass perennially.

But if you had a new bike it was safe with "Briggie," because he stood there and watched them all day. You gave him your tanner and licked a label and stuck it on your saddle and put your bike in a stall, and he gave you the other half of the t ticket so that you'd know your new Raleigh or your Hercules from the hundreds of others that stood in long rows beside it. And if you didn't take the trouble to scrape "Briggie's" label off your saddle folks would know for weeks to come that you had been to Aikey Fair.

And gaen the kitchie-deem was with you you paid for her bike as well, especially if she gave you one of those bewitching smiles that have a sweetness in youth that last you till your old age. Some lads had got the length of a motor-bike and were taking their quines on the back pillion, so maybe you were lucky that this quine had come along with you, because most of them were looking for lads with motor-bikes, to take them away to dances and such like. But you didn't care much for hooching and dancing, and maybe the quine just liked your company, so you took her by the hand up the brae and set her down among the heather bells, and you thought she was the finest picture in all the fair.

There was a kind of sparkle in her soft eyes that was maybe worth more than diamonds, especially if you didn't care much for money, and a velvet gloss on her hair as it tumbled about in the

sun glint, with maybe a bit coloured ribbon in it, tryin' to
beguile a daft gowk like yourself that had been looking all the
week at a mare's tail tied up with segs.

She had a straw hat with a red band and a checked tweed
coat, but as it was a stifling day these lay beside her on the
heather; and there she sat with bare arms in a print frock, net
stockings and brown brogue shoes, her smiling lips reminding you
of a combed honey and a scent about her like carnations, shy
and blushing as a sunrise.

You must have looked an awful gowk yourself sitting there
in your best blue suit and an open collar white sark you had
borrowed from the third horseman; hand-sewn brown shoes
that were far too dear but suited your vanity, even a watchchain across your waistcoat and your hair oiled and parted in
the middle; your Bogie-roll left at home in your kist and
smoking a long-stemmed Sunday pipe filled with scented
tobacco.

Ah well, when you'd had your fill of looking at the quine
and listening to the music of her laugh, and maybe stealing
a kiss on the sly, you'd take her hand again and you'd dander
down to the fair to see the sights and maybe listen to the pipe
bands. She was quiet like your quine and didn't have much to
say, and you liked her all the better for this, so she took her
coat on her arm and her hat in her hand and down the brae
you'd go, the soft wind playing with her hair and her voice a
timid whisper.

But you couldn't hear each other speaking for the din of the
carnival, the hurdy-gurdy organ on the chair-o-planes grinding
out "That Ole Black Mammy o' Mine," and the chairs loaded
with screaming quines swinging out over your heads. But you
soon discovered that your quine wouldn't go on any of the
whirligigs; she wasn't going to have her legs swinging out in the
air above the gaping crowds, she was far too shy for that, so
you took her to see the Death Riders on their Wall of Death,
clinging to their motor-bikes like flies in a jar, screaming up
nearly to the rim of the giant barrel when they were at full speed,
their tyres nearly touching your toes where you stared down at
them from the railing. Three motor-bikes were on the wall at

one time, with a game bit quine on the pillion of one of them,
flying round and round like a bool in a brose caup, the roar
of their engines like to deafen you and the speed of their
machines shaking the wooden structure under your feet, while
all the time you were feart that they flew over the top of the
wall. But eventually, when they felt you'd had your money's
worth they snorted down their bikes and descended to the
grass circle, when everybody threw down pennies to the riders,
because it was said that no insurance company would take them
on at such a risk. This was above your admission money, and
maybe it was just a gimmick, but you felt it was worth it
and you threw your meck with the others, maybe a tanner
if you felt big hearted.

So you came down the steps from the tower of death and
went and had a bit keek at one of Cleopatra's handmaidens
who had been in a trance for two-thousand years, though you
would have liked to pinch her in the right places to make
sure. But you wondered how they had managed to feed the
creature all these years, and a lot of other things that entered
your head as you looked at her under her silken veil. She was
the colour of faded lilies; smooth as wax, cold as death, not a
tremble on her eyelids, and her breathing wouldn't have stirred
a feather. She was the picture of a living corpse, if such a
thing could be.

In another tent a pirate-looking lad was throwing knives at a
quine nearly naked, just missing her fair skin by the breadth of
your finger nail. But you couldn't spend all your penny-fee on
the side shows; on the penny arcades, the spinning wheel,
the fortune-tellers, the fat woman or the midget, on the ghost
train or the coconut shies, the shooting galleries or the
Chep-Johns, so after a squint at yourselves in the contorting
mirrors you'd buy an ice-cream cone for yourself and one
for your quine. And you'd listen for a while to the evangelists
preaching repentance to the sinners, reminding the ill-gotten
creatures that the Kingdom of God was at hand, or that the end
of the world was in sight, with all the fire and brimstone,
till they had your quine nearly frightened to death, listening
to all that stite, for you knew fine it wasn't the way religion

should be taught, so you took her away.

When you'd finished licking your cone you took a swing with the mallet to see if you could ring the bell at the top of the pole, but for all the fencing posts and sheep-stakes you had driven into the yird you couldn't manage it, and maybe it served you right for trying to show off in front of the quine. But you was a fair hand at ruggin' the swingletree so you would have a pull at the handle on the brass box, where a clock registered your stupid might; but you didn't make much of that either, and you wasn't going to rive at the thing or you ruptured yourself.

You had just got your breath back when who should appear but the old shepherd from Scrapehard, where your father was cottared, the first time you had seen the man without a crook, or his dogs at heel, Rip and Fanny, and he was fair taken with your quine and said he would tell your mither he had seen you with a lass at Aikey Fair. Not that you cared a damn for this but you were a bit bashful with the quine and didn't want to be seen by more folk of your acquaintance than you could help, so you went away up the hill again, out of the steer, for if you want to meet folks you haven't seen for half-a-century go to Aikey Fair, and if they aren't dead you are almost certain to find them on the brae.

You didn't care much for drink but you'd buy a bottle of ginger-beer and a packet of Abernethy biscuits and you'd have a bit picnic up on the hillside, away from the noise and the sweat, where there was peace and quiet, and you could look at the beauty of your quine against the pine trees and the pale summer sky.

So after your ale and biscuits you took this bit slip of a quine up to see the Druids' Circle on the summit of Aikey Brae, where it overlooks Crichie and the lands of Pitfour and Aden, Saplinbrae and Bruxie, and you explain to the quine what you know about the Druids and their weird circles of standing stones that are thousands of years old, and you tell her that under certain circumstances, peculiar to the Druids, she might have been slaughtered on the alter stone as a sacrifice to the Sun God, while the Druid priests stood around chanting in their

84

white robes and smearing her blood on the stones.

The blood-thirsty creatures must have had a gie chauve to get these monoliths dragged up the hill at Aikey and hoisted on their ends in geometrical formation, for the mathematicians would have us believe that their formation has something to do with astronomy, or the measuring of time, like a sundial, because the Druids set their stones to catch the noon-day shadows in the same position in most of their circles, and if that be so the Druid circles were the first clocks in existence, long before the sand-glass.

So you are fair engrossed with the Druid creatures and their blood rites and orgies and the quine thinks that you must be daft or something to be so taken up with a circle of lintel stones that could have been set up on their ends for the nowt to scratch their hides on. Maybe some day she'd learn to share your thoughts, but in the meantime she chides you for tearing her fine net stockings on the whins and briars that grew on the hillside.

Oh aye, she'd heard about the Pict creatures being converted by that Saint Drostan chiel that had landed at Aberdour, there had been a picture about it in her school book; and there was that kirk in Auld Deer that had been biggit in his name. Abody kent aboot that. Did you think she was a dunce? So you tells her about the Monks of Deer and the ancient Book of Deir they had written in Gaelic about religion; written out by in yon rickle of stones that used to be the grand Abbey of Deer, before the laird of Pitfour carted most of it away to build his steadings. She said you should have been a minister or something, and not just a farming chiel, and you laughed at this and said that you wasn't a bit religious, it was just that you liked to know the history of the place. But you couldn't help telling her that she was standing on one of the most sacred spots in all Scotland, what you might call the cradle of our religion, where the Pagan and the Saint have left their mark.

And you told the quine about the Holy Fair that the Monks had started for the relief of the poor and the upkeep of their Abbey; the Holy Day which became a local hol(i)day and was the real beginning of the Fair but was named after the tink who fell into the Ugie with his pack or got soaked in the rain and spread his trinkets to dry on the Brae. And the folks on their way to Old Deer bought all the trock that Aikey had spread out in the blink of sun between the thunder pelts. So Old Aikey came back again next year on the same day with a huge pack on his back, almost all that he could stagger with, and he spread it out on the heather and the passers-by bought every knick-knack that he had. Then the old fool went away and got drunk and told all the other hawkers about the folks at Old Deer that were daft about strings of beads and silk scarfs and brooches and such like, so the next year a great birn of tinks came to Aikey's Brae and some of them sold their shelts to the farming chiels and that was the start of the horse market. Syne the gypsies came with their caravans and their fortune-tellers and their travelling clowns and before long you had a real jamboree on the hillside.

You wasn't sure how it got started on the Sunday, but maybe it was because the tinks came at the week-end to get their stalls up for the Wednesday, and when there were so many ill-mannered creatures standing about watching they might as well sell them something, so they got yoked on the Sunday.

Now that there were motor cars folk came from far and wide to Aikey. The railway folk had even started running trains on a Sunday for the Fair, and they had built a halt anent the Abbey of Deer to let the heathens walk up to the steer that was on the hill. They said it was to accommodate the clergy that wanted to visit the old abbey once in a while, and you wouldn't deny that there were some creatures in long black frock-coats that came off the train on a Sunday, and you supposed that they were Monks though they minded you on Hoodie-craws that went trooping over the field to the ruin of an abbey, where a bit brig had been erected to let them over the Ugie. And they thought they were there for a benediction until they whips out their fishing-rods from under their frocks and hardly leaves a trout or a salmon in the Ugie for a common body. And the pokes and bores around this cairn of an abbey till you thinks they have taken up residence in the place, reading great screeds of poetry and chanting out loud until you are fair deaved and feart to go near the place in the dark. They nearly put you off poaching these unearthly creatures and you could say that there was hardly any need for a Water Baillie while they were moaning around in the woods.

And here was Jamie Sutherland scrubbing the herring scales off his motor-lorries and fitting them out with forms for seats and a tarpaulin cover for a hood, tearing out and into Peterheid with passengers for the Fair, though mostly on the Wednesday for fear of offending the fisher folk. The smell of herring and petrol made them an exciting experience and next day you could see the same lorries back at the pier with their herring barrels. They said that Jamie Sutherland bought his first Clydesdale at Aikey Fair, and that next year he went up with one horse and came back with seven.

And yon Sandy Burnett from Mintlaw, him that left the ploo at Lunderton and went and bought a bus to drive folks to Aikey, and look at him now with three or four of them on the road, and likely to get more of them as every Aikey goes by.

But you had blethered long enough about Aikey, so you took the quine by the hand and went linking down the brae to the fair again. Hunger had taken the quine, and as you were a bit jaded yourself you went into a tent for your tea. A lot of people were leaving the fairground, so you went and got your bicycles out of "Briggie's" park, but the road was fair jammed with folk and you had to walk nearly all the way to Old Deer, where the drunks were stitering about in front of the Aden Arms Hotel, and a lad was nearly feart to go by lest they pull your quine off her bicycle.

Next day you'd get all the banter from the other lads for taking the deem away to Aikey, and they'd tease the quine about it too at dinner time; but you didn't care a damn, and neither did she, for something had sprung up between you which made you sacred to each other, whatever they said, and a wink on the sly was a bond of understanding, until such time as you had the chance to seal it with a kiss, in glad remembrance of Aikey Brae.

FOLKS IN BLACK

Life can be a wearisome business for a five-year-old girl especially when all the bairns next door have gone off to school and there is no one left to play with. I was now age for school but mother said I would have to wait until after the summer holidays. My school-bag and slate had already been bought, and a sliding box to hold slate-pencils, varnished with a flower on the lid, but what good were these if I couldn't have them to show off with.

I had lost all interest in my stocking-dolls and weaving "cattie's tails," and what good were "hoosies and lames" without someone to share them with, or even skipping and "beddies" without a partner? I was getting big enough to play these games but they just weren't any good on your own.

I had become so frustrated with myself that I started to bite my nails. Then I got a skelp on the lug from my father and he said: "Ye'll ken what that's for, ma bonnie quinie!" I wasn't sure that I did but it cured me of nail-biting for life, besides making my eyes water and setting the bells ringing in my ears at the time.

So there was little else I could do but run barefoot around the doors of our thatched hovels, which were the cottar houses at Gowanlea, where my father and the foreman lived and worked on the farm. The orra pail stood at our doorstep, where it served as a sink for slop or dishwater, and meantime there was just enough water in it to cover the bottom. I kept dipping my foot in the pail and ran up the close to see how much sand I could collect on my sticky sole.

Megan Handerson, who was my mother, stood watching my antics, while she leaned on the door jamb, her arms folded, waiting for the tatties to boil for the dinner. The folk next door called her Mrs. Stoddart, but Handerson was her own name and she liked it better.

Dave Rafferty, our Irish foreman lived next door, and at this moment he came round the corner for his mid-day meal. He had a large family and he poached for rabbits half the night to keep them alive. When all else was at rest Dave would be out with ferret and nets, while the stars sparkled and the whin dykes glistened with frost.

But when Dave Rafferty saw mother standing in the cottage door he stopped.

"Aye lass," he said, "I heard ye comin' hame this mornin'. Ye made an affa noise hammerin' on the door tae wauken Charlie."

Charlie was my father's name, Charles Stoddart, and he was the stockman on the farm.

"Aye," Megan replied, "Charlie had the door barred on the inside and I couldna get in. He doesna like tae bide 'imsel unless the door is barred. But what time was that, Dave?"

"Oh, aboot one o'clock, mebbee."

"Weel, ye see, I was at my father's place and I was late or I got hame on ma bike. I had tae rap hard on the door for Charlie tae lat me in."

"Weel lass, I was richt glaed tae hear ye knockin', 'cause it waukened me frae an ugly dream. I dreamed that folks in black were tryin' tae get a coffin in at your door and it wadna go. They tried hard tae get it in at your door but it wadna go. They kicked up an affa noise and I fair thocht they had yer door doon. And when they saw they couldna get the coffin in at your door they cam' up the close wi' it tae me; a black coffin wi' toshils on't, I saw it fine. That must hae been when I heard ye bangin' on the door. But what pleased I was when I kent it was only a dream."

"It must hae been the nichtmare ye had," said Megan.

"Na lass, it's yersel' that tak's the nichtmare. Charlie tells me he has tae hide the key every nicht tae keep ye frae goin' ootside in yer nichtgoon. He said there was ae nicht ye was tearin' the hair oot o' the lassie's heid there, and that ye thocht at the time ye was pluckin' a hen. I'll bet it had been damned sair, eh quine!" And he patted my head for approval.

Megan laughed at this. "Oh aye," says she, "but there was anither nicht that I was bashin' the pram against the room door ben the lobby. I thocht it was a barra, and that I was a quine again and muckin' oot ma father's byre, and that I couldna get the barra up the midden plank. It's a wonder that ye didna hear me that nicht Dave."

"And a blessin' that I didna lass. Weel, I'll awa' tae ma denner or the tatties will be caul'. Charlie's late the day. He's surely been hindered wi' the kye. I think the roan coo was like tae calve this mornin'."

"We'll get new cheese than."

"I dinna like the stuff lass."

"Nae even wi' raisins in't?"

"No lass, I'd raither hae a bowl o' yerned melk ony day."

Dave Rafferty walked up the close to his dinner. I dipped my foot in the pail at the doorstep and followed him gathering sand on my wet sole as I went along. While my back was turned Megan came to the door to "bree the tatties," and she strained off the scalding water into the pail, shook the tattie pot and went back into the house. When my foot had dried off I came hopping back to the doorstep and plunged my naked foot into the steaming pail. Then I fairly yelled in agony, and my scream brought Megan back to the door. When my father came round the corner I was dancing on one foot, yelling like mad, while the other was seared nearly to the bone.

About a fortnight later Dave Rafferty was wracked with a hach and a hoast that put him off his work with pneumonia, while I had developed blood-poisoning from my scalded foot. Dave had been poaching for rabbits half the night for a week, sitting out in the cold and the wet till he was fair chilled to the bone. He had no strength left in his legs and came out in a sweat and cold shivers till he was forced to take to his bed. Eight or nine rowdy bairns ran back and forth in the dark lobby or hung around his shabby bed. The man could get no rest for his own bairns and he tossed and turned in his bed till he was ravelled in the head.

The doctor came and had a look at him and sounded his chest and said he should be poulticed, back and front, and gave orders that a bottle of turpentine be mixed with the potion to keep it warm. He also prescribed a mixture, and took one of the older quines back with him to the town to get these things from a chemist, which was a brave thing for the doctor to do because the creature was itching with lice. But before he did this he came in by and had a look at my swollen foot, which also had to be poulticed, and said he would look in again sometime.

Dave Rafferty's wife was almost witless in her perplexity and the house stank with neglect. Her man got worse in the night and asked for his medicine. She got up from his side in the box-bed and fumbled in the candlelight for the physic. What with worry and want of sleep she was on the brink of distraction, so she just poured out a doze from the nearest bottle on the mantleshelf. Dave didn't like his medicine, so he swallowed it at a gulp. The hot liquid seared his gullet and made him cough and retch. He twisted his face and shuddered at the taste of it.

"Ye stupid bitch," he spluttered, "you've given me turpentine."

"Turpentine," said his wife, and looked at the stained label on the bottle. "Michty mee! What'll I dee?"

So what does the frantic woman do but comes hammering on our door at the dead of night with her bloodless fists, even worse than Megan was doing on the night that Dave dreamed about the folks in black coming up the close with his coffin.

"Oh let me in," she cried, "Dave's worse, much worse, oh let me in!" And it seemed she would have the door in staves by the time Megan got out of bed to open it.

She swept in upon us like a ghost from a whirlwind, with a shawl over her nightgown, barefooted, and her black hair was blown about her white, scared face.

"It's murder I tell ye, murder," she cried, clutching her shawl, "I've poisoned my man with turpentine and he's stark raving mad. Oh Mrs. Stoddart, I couldna help it. I took the wrang bottle frae the mantlepiece and he just gulped it doon.

91

He's dyin' I tell ye, and it was me that poisoned 'im, his ain wife. Oh, what'll I dee? Mrs. Stoddart. What'll I dee?"

She was sobbing hysterically and fell into Megan's arms like a heart-broken schoolgirl.

"But turpentine's nae rank poison woman," Megan remonstrated. "It winna kill yer man. Maybe it's made him drunk, like whisky. He'll be a' richt or mornin'. I'll come roon and we'll gie him a dose o' castor oil and he'll soon sleep it aff."

"Oh na na, Mrs. Stoddart, he's waur than ye think. He took a gie big doze o' turpentine. Will ye go for the doctor? — juist tae ease my mind."

So Megan dressed herself and cycled six miles to the town to see the doctor. Charles wouldn't go on his bike after dark.

The doctor lived in a posh part of the town, where trees grew out of the pavements, and every house had a front garden. The street lamps were out and Megan could hardly see the brass knocker on his varnished door.

She rattled the heavy knocker and the doctor peeped out from a window on the roof.

"What do you want at this time of night?" he snapped.

"I'm Mrs. Stoddart from the hovels at Gowanlea. Do you mind on Dave Rafferty, the foreman there? You've been attending him for pneumonia."

"Yes, I remember, Mrs. Stoddart. I'm sorry I was so rude with you. But what is the trouble?"

"Well, Mrs. Rafferty has given her man a dose of turpentine in mistake for his medicine and she thinks he's goin' tae die. He's ravin' mad and she thinks she's poisoned him. She wants ye tae come at once doctor."

"Delirious eh! And no wonder, after a dose of turpentine. Probably it has raised his temperature a little but it wont do him any real harm. Tell the woman to give her man a good stiff dose of castor oil and I'll be out first thing in the morning. And keep the poultice going. By the way, Mrs. Stoddard, how is your wee girlie's foot?"

"It's terribly swollen and she's affa lame."

"I can't hear you."

Megan repeated her statement in a louder voice and it seemed she would wake the whole street.

"Very well, if it's ripe tomorrow — today, I mean, I'll lance it. But don't tell the wee lass; we'll break it to her gently. Good-Morning! Mrs. Stoddart."

The doctor's head disappeared and the window went down with a clash. The light went out in his room and Megan was left in the darkness.

Mrs. Rafferty gave her man a dose of castor oil and he quietened down a bit. He fell asleep in a stupor and talked nonsense. Megan sat beside his bed and his wife quietened the bairns. She got them all to sleep ben the hoose and fell asleep herself in the midst of them.

But Dave began to chauve again, tossing the blankets nearly out of the bed, trying to get out of a load of straw he had toppled in the farm close. Syne Gip and Fanny had bolted at the ploo and he fair tugged at the sheets trying to pull them in. He was hot and steamy and tossed about restlessly on the bed. Megan dipped a cloth in cold water and swabbed his face and temples. Eventually he lapsed into unconsciousness and Megan left the damp cloth on his brow, rinsing it now and then in cold water and replacing it on his forehead.

Megan somehow knew that Dave Rafferty had reached the crisis of his illness. Very soon he would die, or show signs of improvement. . . . . .

Mrs Rafferty got up at daybreak and made tea. But Megan couldn't relish it. The smell of the dirty hovel made her squeamish, and already she thought she felt the itch of lice. Not that Megan really blamed the woman, for she didn't have a chance with all that bairns.

That day at noon, when my father came home for dinner, Megan ran up the close to speir for Dave Rafferty. He seemed somewhat revived but showed only the whites of his eyes under heavy lids.

Megan bent over him. "Do you know me? Dave," she asked.

"Aye lass, I ken ye fine. Folks in black were tryin' tae get a coffin in at your door but it wadna go. They — they tried hard tae get it in at your door but it wadna go — so they cam' up the close wi' it tae me. . . . ."

93

His words were mumbled from between cracked swollen lips and the effort exhausted him. Megan ignored what he said and bent over him again.

"Are ye feelin' ony better Dave?" she asked.

"Oh aye," he seched, "a wee bittie." But his eyes were glazed with death. He turned his face to the wall and fell into another troubled sleep. Megan felt his pulse. It was weak, almost indiscernible, and his breathing came in short faint gasps that brought pink froth to his lips.

"The doctor's comin' back in the efterneen," his wife said.

Two hours later Dave Rafferty was dead. His wife lay over him and wept sorely. She kissed his pallid face and her hot tears ran down his cheeks. Megan took her away from the bed and set her on a chair. The younger of the bairns cried when they saw their mother greetin'. The others gathered round her chair, silent and wide-eyed.

"Yer father's deid," the mother sobbed, "and I poisoned him. I poisoned him, bairns, d'ye hear!"

Megan shook her by the shoulders. "Ye didna poison 'im' woman. Get that oot o' yer heid afore it takes root. Never mind her, bairns, she's haverin'; she didna poison yer dad — he was goin' tae die onywye."

When the doctor had finished with Dave Rafferty he set me on Megan's knee and lanced my foot. He flicked the ugly swelling with a lancet and squeezed out the thick bluish matter with his thumbs.

Megan looked away for a moment. "Could it be dangerous? doctor," she asked.

"Not now, Mrs Stoddart, but had we not managed to localise the poison, with the help of poultice, and had the infection got into the girl's bloodstream, I wouldn't care to say what might have happened. . . . But you're going to be all right now my wee girl."

He washed my foot in hot water and swathed it tightly in a bandage. He set me on the rug by the fire and ruffled my brown ringlets. "You've been a brave little girl," he said, closed his leather bag with a snap, put on his hat and departed.

"Bye bye!" he said.

Megan went to the door and watched him as he walked down the close to his car, an old "Tin Lizzie" with a canvas hood. She watched the dust rising from the wheels of the doctor's car until it disappeared on a bend of the road. I was standing beside her on one foot, still reeking of lysol, and holding on to her long skirts.

Megan turned her head and looked towards the Rafferty's door. She could see the hens pecking around the doorstep but there was no sign of the bairns. Their drab shabby blinds would be down though the sun was shining so beautifully. It would be eerie now to come home late at night and bang on the cottage door. Now that Dave Rafferty was gone Megan felt afraid of the dark.

She bent down and her strong young arm went round my shoulders. In a moment she had gathered me close to her warm skirts and was smothering my cheeks with her hot tears and kisses.

WHO WOULD BE A GAFFER

YOU had heard about the gaffers in the old days who walked
in at one end of the stable at yoking time and out at the other,
snapping out orders as they went, never dachling, and the men
trying to catch their words in the by going, but feart to back
speir if they didn't, for woe betide a man gaen he back speired
a gaffer in those days. Cairt neeps, ploo and thrash was about the
gist of it in winter; hyow, hay and harvest in the summer months,
with maybe a pucklie o' peats to cast or yows to clip, so you
couldn't go very far wrong with the horse wark, one day was the
same as the next and complications were few; maybe the odd
beltie broken on thrashin days or a colt to yoke in the spring, the
rest was hard work and long hours and you could manage fine
without machinery. For ploomen chiels in those days it was
mostly "Juist haud back again lads and blacken a bittie mair!"
So there wasn't much to be said at yoking time anyway.

   But by the mid-fifties all this was changing and it wasn't so easy
being a gaffer nowadays: what with they new tractors coming in
and the horses disappearing, the changing of implements and
methods, working shorter hours with fewer men; and yet you
were expected to produce the same results as before, or even
better, and at greater speed, because all this new-fangled
machinery had to be paid for.

   The pickiesae hat and the nickie tams were gone forever; so
were the piked hames, the segs and the harness cleaning, and
nowadays you seldom saw a double-cased lever watch or a lad in
tackety boots smoking a "Stonie" pipe and bogie-roll. The old

"heavies" were fast disappearing and a new generation of mechanics were taking their place. The Agricultural Revolution was in full swing and a new image in farming was being created, so different from the old that nowadays you could hardly tell a farm worker from a town billie, except maybe that the country chiel had a bit more colour in his face. Some of them even had motor cars, which didn't give the toon bairns a chance to run after them crying:

"Country Geordie, Brig o' Dee,
Sup the brose and leave the bree!"

as they had done with their fathers.

The old gaffers were on the way out too. Those who were still carrying on were sending men to jobs they couldn't do themselves, and unless they could drive a tractor they were getting in the way. Farmers wanted a "working" grieve who could handle machinery and take his turn with a tractor. But you had foreseen this and could whip a tractor about with the best of them, although they got a laugh at you for a start, especially when you tried to back it into the shed with a load of sheaves or turnips, but it had been well worth while to persist.

And you could just see yourself stamping into the tractor garage snapping out orders at men dressed in berets and boiler suits, duffle coats and wellington boots; men who had scarcely ever seen a horse yoked, and one of them had asked you what the saddle-trees were for in the old stable. When you told the foreman what to do he immediately kicked up his tractor and the others couldn't hear for the noise, or see you for the diesel fumes, so you had to shout in their ears till you nearly choked, while they consulted their wrist watches to make sure you wasn't a minute too soon. Yoking half-a-dozen horse teams was a pleasure compared with this rumpus, and if you didn't jump out of the way quick they would run you over; what with their haversacks and tea flasks you would think they were off for the day, not just a few short hours and the rest overtime.

You just couldn't imagine what your old man would have thought of this lot; them with their half-days on Saturdays and summer holidays with pay, and never a wet sark sitting in their

97

tractor cabs. Some change from the old days when it was
"stracht theets" for ten hours a day, up at five in the morning
and back to supper-up in the evening, and never a bite to eat
between meals. This crowd never rose or the "postie" was by,
and their winter day was that short you sometimes wondered how
you was going to get everything fitted in. But maybe it was for
the better, because some of the men were old before their time
in the old days, wracked with work and rheumatism, and never
knew what it was to get a holiday beyond the feeing market
or a term day.

But the weather was still the real master as it had always been:
even with all their contraptions they hadn't managed to alter that
or get the weather to suit the wark. Yesterday you was at the
hay-makin' but the rain came on and spoiled it, so you had to
send the men inside to scrub the "dry coo" byre. Today the
rain had ceased but the hay was conached for the present,
rather a pity because it was well matured and almost ready for
stacking. Just shows how many irons you must have in the fire
at a time like this, and being the gaffer you got to give the men
a job: you can't have them digging holes in the ground just
to fill them in again to pass the time, the manager would think
you was off your nut and maybe give you the sack. So in
weather like this you have to have a lot of things going at the same
time, and you've got to keep cool when things go wrong. Of
course you still got the "dry coo" byre to paint after the
scrubbing, and there's a great heap of coiryarn in the loft to be
unravelled and wound into balls. You just threw it aside when
you took it off the stacks in the winter time, but you have to
get it all ready again for the hairst. A while back you could
have the men inside to twine strae rapes on a rainy day, but
that's all past now and the thraw heuks are thrown aside, now
that you've got nets or "hackles" for covering the rucks.

Being a gaffer you've got a lot more things to think about
than the other lads. But you are supposed to be able to crack a
joke just the same. You're not supposed to go about with a face
that would sour the mannie's milk just because the weather
has gone against you. You get bigger paid to carry a lot more in
your mind than the other chiels, and if your head is screwed on

the right way you should manage it, otherwise you shouldn't be
a gaffer. Of course you get the blame for everything but you've
got a skin as thick as a nowt beast and you can thole it; and what
the men say about you behind your back would make you cock
your lugs in your sleep. Not that you lose a blink of sleep over
it, 'cause you've learned to trample a lot of the stite under
your feet. Damnit man, if you was to listen to all their yammer
you would be awake for twenty-four hours a day, and not fit
to take a bite of meat for the thought of it. Just because you
was a gaffer you knew some folk that would have you on
crutches and your wife up the wall, your family all in prison
or in hospital, and if looks were anything to go by you should
freeze in your boots or go up in a blue flame. But your father
was a gaffer before you and you'd learned from him how to settle
their hash.

And you had thon manager chiel to contend with, not that
he was a bad stock, but he always wanted to know the outs and
ins of everything and you had to keep him informed. He had
even tried you to keep a diary about what the men were doing
every day, but you had drawn the line at this and said that gaen
you had wanted a job as a clerk you wouldn't be here. Him and
his beuks, and all this fash about having everything down on
paper. That was college folk for ye, but you had told the
creature what he could do with his diary, every flippin' page of
it, and you thought he was offended. But that was a long time
back and the manager had learned since then that you had
a crackin' good memory and could manage fine without a
pencil behind your lug.

The manager had come straight out of college, with nothing
but what he stood in by way of clothes, and riding a bicycle;
but brim full of fancy ideas, and you had to put him in his place
from time to time, or he would have everything growing upside
down and all out of season. Not that the man hadn't wit,
and he had shown a lot of folk out by that there was more in him
than the spoon put in, for it's little they thought of him when he
first came to the place. That creature they said will never
manage an estate of that size; he's got it all out of books and he'll
find it a different thing when he puts his ideas into practice.

But he had opened their eyes the breet, and them that shunned him for a start would now like to pass the time of day over the dyke, but he was a man by himself and wouldn't listen to any of their claik.

And you had to admit that the manager had changed a lot of things and brought the farms really up to date: what with that braw new milking parlour and press-button milking at the Home Farm; the new tattie sheds he had biggit, and big fodder barns that held nearly a' the crap under a roof, so that ye had little bother getting everything inside from the weather. The way he was going he would soon have the whole steading under glass, like a hot house, stacked with manure and implements. You never saw such a creature for manure and you guessed that for every bag of corn or tatties that went away a sack of manure came back. It soon would be that you could manure the grun on an ordinar fairm with the soil of this place. The kye were wading to their bellies in grass but still he stoured it on, and the hay was that rich you could hardly cure it. A "controlled surplus" he called it but you hardly knew what the creature meant, though it was true that the farms were running more milk, corn and tatties than you had ever seen before.

He wasn't feared of work either the stock, manager though he was, skelpin' on in his shirt sleeves from daylight to dark, with nothing on his head, working all day and writing in books half the night, it made you feel half affronted for the little you did in comparison. Talk about a collar-and-tie job; if this man put on a collar he would choke himself, or hang himself with the tie, for he always had his sark neck open nearly to his navel. The man hardly slept either, just a few hours on the pillow after his clerking and he was up in the morning and into the dairy

byre as if the place belonged to him. You never saw such a man for work and he fair made a hobby of it: never had time for a smoke or a drink, or a bit hooch of a dance and how he got hold of that slip of a quine for a wife you would never know. Over six feet he was and you had to look up to the man, more ways than one, and behind that ready smile of his was an awful lot of thinking. But maybe it would tell on him some day, for his

hair was grey already for a young man, and cropped short as
stubble.

You knew fine that the manager was more popular with the
men that you was; and no wonder, for since the firm gave him
that motor car he was never slack to take their wives to the
houdi, day or night, and blin' drift made no difference for then
he took a tractor; always ready to do a good turn, though
sometimes he got little thank for it, and if he could't speak
good of a man he held his tongue. But you always remembered
that time when you was off work and the manager took your
place, and when you came back the men were all on about the
manager: it was the manager did this and the manager said
that until you were fair deaved with their clipe. But they didn't
know him quite as well as you did, or maybe they wouldn't
have been so verty, for he said things to you that they didn't
hear, and as he had an eye for each man's work individually he
wasn't slack to say what he thought of it, for he wasn't above
a bit of honest criticism.

But sometimes the lad took things in his head that just had
to be dealt with, even though it was only to show that you was
still the gaffer; like that time at the start o' hairst when he came
home from the town in a great fizz because everybody on the
way out was cutting their corn and you wasn't started. He
had nearly run into a bus from gawking at all the binders tearing
round the parks and nothing done at home. You had the men out
cleaning ditches at this time of year and maybe he thought they
should be clearing roads for the binders. So he comes to you in a
great flurry and asks why aren't you started man? Everybody's
cutting from here to the toon! You thought of asking him that
if all these people jumped into the harbour in the toon, would
he jump in after them? But you thinks this would be a bit
impudent, so you puts your pipe away and calmly tells the man
that the stuff isn't ready for cutting. But he doesn't believe you
and wants to know why, thinking maybe that you are a bit
thrawn; so you takes him to the gate of a corn field and tells
him to go in there and fill his oxter with the stuff, and when
he had it all together in his arms it was as green as kale. With
that he apologised for his rashness and said he wouldn't have

101

believed it any other way. It would look mighty green in a stook you say, especially if you are going to thrash early as you usually do; man it would hardly weigh in a sack and you would never get them tied. He admits this and then you slyly tells him that he still has a lot to learn though he has been to the college.

And there was that other time in the spring during the war when the neep seed was that scarce you couldn't get it at any price. But you had a few pounds of old turnip seed in the loft, a wee bit musty but you knew fine it would grow in fair weather and the ground in trim. So you shows this little sack to the manager and he shakes his head and says you cannot sow that stuff because it is too old and wizened looking and will never take root. Too big a risk he says and you might lose the crop. You tries to reason with the man but he is as stocket as a newly cogged calf, when round the corner comes his bit quine of a wife and says that he is wanted on the 'phone. When the manager's back is turned you take a dander the way of the tractor garage and pours a droppie paraffin in the bag among the neep seed; a daft like thing to do, but just a little makes the seed trickle better through the seed-barrow, besides brightening its colour. You gives the seed a bit stir with your fingers and shakes the bag, and when the manager appears again you show him what he thinks is a different mixture of seed. He pokes his head into the bag and brightens up immediately. You wonder that he doesn't feel the smell of the paraffin, but no; and he puts his hand in the bag and runs the seed through his fingers. He says that is a much better sample grieve and you were lucky to find it and that you can start planting right away. You wait till he is fully convinced and then you tells him it is the same seed and he nearly falls into the brander at his back. He wants to know how you have managed to make it look so fresh, and how you got up to that trick. But you just laughs and shakes your head and hints that he still has a hantle to learn though he had been at the college for a life time.

At the moment however there's still the tatties to rogue and it's about the only thing you will get away with for the time being. But you don't like tattie—roguing, and being the gaffer

you don't have to go with the men on a job like that. That is
one good privilege you've got above the others, in that you can
choose your job, at least to some extent, provided you
haven't a conscience and that you know the best place to hide.
You are blamed for that in any case so you might as well take
full advantage of it so when there's a bit of a hash on or some
heavy lifting to be done you just make yourself scarce, because
though you stuck your neck out and slaved yourself to the
marrow they'd still say the same things about you. So why spoil
a reputation that has served you so well for so long?

So once you get the men yoked to the tattie-roguin'
you could stick your thumbs in your waistcoat and make an
errand down to the blacksmith; not that he will have much time
to listen to your blab, him being busy like, but it will keep you
out of sight for a time, and you could always say that you was
down at the smiddy for yon mower blade that needed sortin'.
What with the second cut of silage comin' on you had to have
a mower blade. Daggit now that just reminded you it's high
time you had the binder canvasses off to the saddler afore the
hairst begins, for most likely they'll be needin' some repairs.
And what with the men's holidays comin' on; neeps tae shim,
tatties to spray, thistles to cut, hay to stack, one thing or
another, so that you began to wonder if ever you would get a
holiday yourself, for you didn't get much peace as a
gaffer.

THE BROKEN SCYTHE —
A STRATAGEM THAT FAILED

BOB LEANED over his scythe and felt the edge of the blade
with his thumb. He referred to the wooden part of his scythe as
the "sned." It resembled a deer's antlers with only two spikes
left for handles, and the wood was gnarled with age and wear
until it looked like polished horn. Resting the scythe on its
"heel" he took a carborundum stone from his belt to sharpen
the blade. Upturning the scythe, now with the antlers under
his oxter, and the point of the sword—like blade on the
ground, Bob began to whet the blunted edge. And now the
clash of stone against ringing steel was echoed in the glade
like the din of battle just begun.

But Bob's enthusiasm didn't match his action. He had about
as much inclination for the work as a fly in a basin of milk.

It was a warm sunny day and the sky was as clear and pure
as a maiden's eye. The clouds were no more than vapours, like
the breath of angels, drifting across the expanse of heaven in
gentle motion. The moisture of the fields was evaporating in
the hot sun, shimmering above the cornfields in a rippling haze.
The corn was rustling in a breathless swoon, hard and ripe and
level with the dykes, ready for harvest.

The skylarks warbled an incessant chorus, mere specks in
the blue that rose and fell in their exuberance of song. From
the pinewood the cushats were cooing a deeper note in the
autumn symphony. Gossamer spangled the grass like fine hairs,
dancing in the sun glint, while the spiders hung their webs on
whin and broom. The air somnolent with the hum of insect and

drone of bee; minty with the fragrance of bogmyrtle.

Bob straddled the burn and slashed at the rushes on the banks. But it was a lazy day, drowsy in the ripeness of autumn — and above all, it was a Saturday, and Bob had expected a half-holiday, the afternoon off from his labours.

But old Weelum the farmer had sent us to cut and bind thatch on the ditch banks, to be ready for the stacks at the end of harvest.

Nowadays the fee-ed loon takes his weekly half-holiday for granted. He does not have to ask it as a favour from his employer: unless he is paid overtime it is there for the taking, a privilege by law, and he doesn't have to trouble himself about excuses for obtaining it.

Forty years ago such a luxury was unheard of, or left to the farmer's discretion, a most disconcerting state of affairs if one was refused a half-day off at the end of a week's hard work, especially if you had a pre-arranged tryst with your quine in some flowery hedgerow, or had planned to attend a football match.

Half-holidays were most common in summer, when the cattle were on pasture, and didn't have to be fed in byres at week-ends. Some farmers gave their men Saturday afternoons off in summer on condition that they worked extra time in harvest without pay. And half-days off were available in slack periods only, mostly between hay-making and harvest, and even then they were scarce if the farmer worked peat. Some of the cottared men (Married men with families) spent their halfdays in the peat-moss, driving home their peat for winter fuel.

But of course there were ways and means of obtaining your freedom on a sunny Saturday afternoon, and many were the subterfuges contrived to secure an occasional half-day off. Sometimes your grandmother died suddenly without any mention of it in the papers; but since you had only two lawful grandmothers, and they had to last a whole summer, you had to space them out a bit. And you didn't worry about the next year as you would probably be moving on among strangers. Grandfathers were not so convenient, as they had a habit of turning up at roups or marts or fee-ing markets, and there was always sure to be somebody who knew them, and who didn't believe in ghosts.

I was only a loon at the time but Bob was a man, still single, and his notion of a half-day off was solely for pleasure. He wanted to ply his fishing-rod from the rocks below the sea-cliffs, with a swirl of gulls mewing overhead, and the silvered waters breaking on the shore. Bob fished at the Bullers of Buchan with an earth-worm on the hook, and many a fine trout he landed for the basket. He took me there one Saturday afternoon after the hay-making. I crawled on my hands and knees to look over the edge of the beetling cliffs. I was terrified, but Bob coaxed me on to follow him, and as I had great faith in Bob I managed to get a foot over the edge. We shinned our way backwards down the Grey Mare ridge, astride the rock, (a position which gave it its name) a leg on each side, our faces to the cliff, Bob with his wand and fishing-bag tied to his back, the two of us like flies above the blue swirl of the waters.

But I didn't stay long on the rocks with Bob. I wasn't interested in fishing and my one concern was to reach the top of the cliff again, alive. Bob wouldn't come back with me, so I had to make it alone, shinning my way up the Grey Mare's back hanging on for dear life, fingering every foothold in a dedicated bid for safety and a longer life. I clung to the hard stone with my whole life in my finger-tips, a huddle of fear between sea and sky, schooling myself not to look back, but to think only of the future and the spine grass at the top of the precipice.

So that was Bob's idea of a holiday. For me it was a nightmare and I would rather have stayed at home — even to gather rushes on the ditch banks, just as we were doing now. . . .

Bob straightened his back and wiped the sweat from his brow with his sleeve. "Ah tae blazes," says he, "Foo can Auld Weelum nae gie us the half-day aff? Sic a fine efterneen for the rock fishin' at that. And wi' the hairst comin' on we winna hae anither chance o' a holiday."

I was gathering the rushes into sheaves, binding them with twisted strands, to be carted away later for the stackyard.

"Foo nae gang hame and ask a halfie then?" I suggested. "It's nae ower late yet!"

Bob kennelt his pipe and spat in the ditch. "Daggit man," says he, "that's nae a bad idea. But first I'll hae tae brak' the scythe, or Weelum will juist send me back tae cut mair thack."

There was no more thatch to gather, so I peeled the green skin from a reed and held up the white cotton-like fibre between thumb and forefinger. "Ken what folk used that for in the old days?" I asked.

Bob looked quizzically at the white fibre. "No loon, I dinna ken what they used it for."

"Well, they dried it and used it for a wick in their oil-lamps tae light their hovels."

"And what has that got tae do wi' us gettin' a halfie?"

"Oh naething," I said, "I just minded on't."

Bob hooked his scythe on to a fencing post and tore out the grass-hook, the small strut that held it together, so that the blade fell away from the handle. In other words, the sword came away from the antlers. "Noo than," says he, mischievously, "the snickle is oot o' the snackle, as they say, and there's nae anither scythe on the premises; they're a' at the smiddy bein' sortet for the hairst."

"And what are ye goin' tae do?" I asked, for I had never seen Bob do anything so reckless.

"You bide here and peel rashes," says he; "I'm gaun awa' hame tae ask Auld Weelum for a halfie, and if I dinna come back I'll send young Weelum tae fetch ye hame."

He shouldered the broken scythe and strode away over the pasture, whistling for the dog. Roy was at his heels in a moment roused from his snooze beneath a golden whin bush. The cattle left their grazing and went after them, curious as they always are at the sight of a dog.

Bob sent the dog at the stirks, snapping at their heels, trying to catch a tail. They disappeared over the hill, Bob and the nowt and the collie, and his bark grew fainter and fainter until they were out of hearing.

It reminded me of a little snatch of a poem we used to recite at school.

"Smock-frock, billy-cock,
Harvest field and hay,
A whistle clear for all the year,
And a heart as fresh as May."

I sat down on the mossy bank, there being no more rushes to bind, and I considered how splendid it would be to have a half-holiday. If I hurried I could still catch most of the afternoon matinee at the pictures. It was so much more exciting than the evening shows when the big folks came. I would have to run three miles to the town, but I would take to the fields for a short-cut. I had done it once before to see "Ben-Hur," and such a splendid experience that had been.

To-day it would be Col. Tim McCoy in "War Paint," and the Indians would be on the war path, tearing over the barren prairies on their piebald chargers, their feathered tiaras streaming in the wind, swinging their gleaming tomahawks and whooping their warbling war cries.

Or they would have a pow-wow with McCoy around the camp fires, smoking the peace-pipe, while their squaws plaited their hair in the wig-wams, for Col. Tim McCoy was a ranger to be reckoned with among the Indians.

In last week's serial Tarzan and Jane had fallen into a lion-trap in the jungle. Now I was dying to know what had happened to them when the hungry lion sprang at them from a corner of the pit.

But my reverie was short-lived when I heard Bob come whistling o'er the lea, the collie at his heels, the cattle prancing behind them.

Some of the stots were challenging Roy to a fight, creeping up behind him, as close as they dared, scraping the earth with their front hoofs and tossing the sods over their backs. But Roy turned and made at them, scattering the whole herd to a safe distance.

Surely we hadn't got a halfie then?

Bob had brought me a can of hot tea and two scones laden with ginger-flavoured rhubarb jam. "Weel loon," says he, "Ye winna be hungry onywye!"

I threw a piece of scone to the collie dog. He snapped it in mid-air, then stood wagging his bushy tail, his head to one side, looking for more.

"Nae luck for a halfie then?" I ventured.

"Daggit man," said Bob, "Weelum was that concerned aboot the scythe bein' broken, and girned sae muckle aboot the cost o' repairs nooadays — man, I juist hadna the he'rt tae seek a halfie."

"Hadna the neck, ye mean!" For my eyes were smarting with disappointment, and a lump was in my throat, which I managed to wash down with the tea.

"Man," says Bob, "It was like kickin' a man efter he was doon; sic a lay-off I got aboot the hardness o' the times he nearly had me in tears."

I pointed with my tea-can at the old rusty scythe he held in his hand. "Where did ye get the Robsorby then?" I asked, that being our Scots name for a scythe, after the maker, Robert Sorby, or some such thing.

"Man," Bob explained, "Weelum had it hidden awa' in the laft yonder, up in the rafters, lyin' amon the cobwebs and the binder canvasses, juist waitin' for somebody tae seek a half-day aff at the start o' hairst. But fegs, it's that blunt (stroking the edge of the blade with his thumb) it wad hardly cut wan o' yer rash wicks, or a print o' butter. Come tae think on't I shouldna hae broken the wan I had!"

"There's midgies noo," I warned, slapping my face with my hand where a midge had bitten me.

"I thocht I felt the buggericks," and Bob lit his pipe to try and dispel them, for the midge doesn't like pipe reek, black twist especially, better known as Bogie-roll.

He whetted the rusty blade and lashed at the bending reeds. "Dammit man, she winna cut at a'. That's your wyte loon! Ye wad put ill inta me, and ye've ruined ma gweed scythe!"

"But I didna tell ye tae brak' the scythe," I protested.

"That was a strategem, and it was the diplomacy that failed. Ae thing leads tae anither, but it was you that set the ba' rollin.'

"Sabotage, I would call it," I said, disconsolately, "and if ye was the ba' ye rolled tae nae purpose!"

"Aye, but ye wad get impudent noo! What aboot the drap tea ye got? Ye wadna hae got that if I hadna gaen hame. But ye'd better come awa' and gether a puckle mair thack, ye've havert lang aneuch noo!"

And so the Indians would have to wait until nightfall before they started their war dance, at least as far as I was concerned; Tarzan and Jane would have to crouch in their lion pit until I saw them rescued.

As for the rock fishing, well, it wasn't much good in the dark. There was always Sunday, as Bob said, but any old man would have told him there was bound to be rain after such a day as this, with all that midges about.

"A' that slammachs on the girse," they would habber from toothless gums, "A' they spider wobs on the whuns; and all that bluddy midgicks aboot, it's bound tae rain!" And "slammachs" by the way was their word for the silver gossamer.

But now a ballet of midges was dancing in the sunhaze, punishing us for our deceit; a thousand hypodermic needles thirsting for our guilty blood.

Every slash of the scythe brought forth a cloud of stinging fury; a curtain of torment that followed us like a shadow, peppering our faces and arms with blistering hot spots.

Bob was raving mad.

"Blast the thing, it winna cut ava. And blast the midgies!" And I echoed his curses.

SARAH AND THE ANGELS

FOLKS said there still were fairies in Lachbeg Woods. Sarah
Blossom, who was my grandmother, had good reason to
remember it, but she swore it was angels she saw that night when
she was in the gig with Gleg. Gleg Handerson was my grandfather,
and he said he didn't see any angels. But he said the shilt saw
something, because it shied and nickered loudly and fell into
the ditch by the roadside. "The geeg lichts gaed oot," said
Gleg," and I couldna see a stime. It was a fine starry nicht and
I was fair blin't wi' a licht as bricht as lichtnin', but ower slow
for that, and it rose up intae the sky." It rose from the hedges,
Sarah confirmed, and it went up to heaven, and she swore
she saw two angels rise in the midst of it, one from each side
of the road, their wings transparent with light.

Megan told me the story a long time ago. Megan was my
mother's name, and she told it to me as a bedtime creepie that
was supposed to keep me out of mischief for days to come. She
had been but a quine at the time and worked on her parents'
farm at Kelpieside, just under the Mattock Hill, with the white
stone deer on its slopes. Gleg had yoked the shilt early after
supper and set off with Sarah in the gig. They were to spend the
evening with the Blossoms, Sarah's folks, away up in the
Strath where the burnie tumbled doon from the hill; where
the troot loupit silver – like in the moonlight and the whaups
wheebled over the segs.

"Bick-birr, bick-birr," the moorhens cried, "g'wa' hame,
g'wa' hame."

111

It was still daylight when Gleg and Sarah left home. Soon they were in Lachbeg Woods, with the laird's dyke on one side and a hedge on the other. The shilt was at a brisk trot and Sarah was well wrapped up in her tartan plaid, a rug on her knees and her hands in a muff. It was almost dark under the trees, but Sarah had sharp eyes, and as the shilt jogged along she spotted an old jacket lying by the roadside; perhaps it had fallen from a cart, or some forester had lost it. "Look Daw," she said to Gleg, for she always called him Daw as the bairns did, "Look Daw, that jacket lyin' on the road; if it's still there when we get back we'll stop and pick it up – it micht fit ye Daw!"

Sarah knew fine that Gleg wouldn't have stopped at the first telling anyway. He would have to make up his mind about a thing like that; him deep in his thoughts of kye and parks, ploughin' and sowin', and a woman was always nagging about something. But Sarah would have him prepared for it on the way home, and she would remind him to stop for the jacket, a pity to leave it lying there . . . . .

But by and by they were up in the Strath and nearing the heather. Partridges that were startled from their nests whirred over the darkening moor, clucking their displeasure of the intruders.

"Bick-birr, bick-birr, g'wa' hame, g'wa' hame," the moorhens cried.

But Gleg never heeded them. It was a return visit that was lang overdue he said. "And forbyes, auld Basil's bottle would be fu' again, and we'll juist gang owerby and gie 'im a hand tae teem't."

"Bick-birr, bick-birr, g'wa' hame, g'wa' hame, g'wa' hame, g'wa' hame."

"Noisy brutes," Gleg mused, and clicked his tongue at the shilt.

Meanwhile at home Megan had her hands full. Being the eldest, she was left in charge, and besides looking after her younger brothers and sisters, she had to milk the kye, sieve the milk and wash the pails; the calfies had to get a suppie in the coggie, and she had to see to the supperin' o' the horse, Kate and Nell, and fasten in the hens. And the deuks had to be chased hame frae the dam or they wad lay awa' in the mornin'.

But Megan's biggest worry was Jancey and Teenie, her two
baby sisters who had not been well lately. Jancey was nearly
two years old and Teenie six months. Before leaving, Sarah had
told Megan to give them their mixtures and put them to bed in
the kitchen. But Jancey had coughed all evening and Teenie had
whimpered and fretted since Sarah had shut the door on them.

It was dark by eight o'clock and Megan lit the paraffin lamp
that hung from the roof and pulled down the blind. Jonas her
brother was two years younger than Megan. Sometimes they
fought, but mostly when they were alone they were friends.
Jonas was afraid of being alone in the dark and trusted her
completely. So when she had the others in bed she lit a lantern
and Jonas carried it to the byre for the milking, while Megan
took the pails.

Jonas hung the lantern on a wire from the rafters and waited
while Megan milked the kye. It was eerie in the byre without
Sarah about the place; spooky too, and Jonas could hardly wait
or the cows were milked. He was suspicious of every lurking shadow
and paced back and forth on the cobblestones, disturbing the
beasts. But he was afraid to go back to the house alone in the
dark. Megan said he would see a ghost in the close. She was
fear't hersel' and couldn't let him go, so she threatened to
blow out the lantern and leave him in the dark. In this way
she could master Jonas and got him to fall to and help her give
the calves their milk.

The milkhouse was as cold as a tomb and fitted with blue
stone shelves like a mortuary. Their shadows flickered
grotesquely on the white-washed walls, enormous silhouettes
out of all proportion to their normal size. The air was damp and
cold, like the smell of a crypt, a cold dead smell, but in hot
weather this place kept the milk from souring. Megan strained
the hot milk into the wide brown earthenware basins that stood
on the shelves. She went to the kitchen for boiling water to
scald the pails, and while she was gone Jonas helped himself
from a cheese kebbuck, crawling with mites.

Next to the stable to give the mares a drink and an oxterful
of hay. Megan held the warm lantern over her head while Jonas

went cannily up to Kate. He was hardly able to lift her pail of water into the manger and she had to get two fills of his small oxter of hay. But Kate and Nell were quiet mares and they knew the touch of Jonas' hand and the sound of his voice. He shook down their bedding with a fork and gave them each a swede turnip, because his father said it was "gweed for their teeth tae humch a neep!"

Back in the house Teenie still girned. Megan gave her the mixture in her milk and rocked her in the cradle. But she wouldn't take the teat on the bottle and screwed her small face into an orgy of pain. The rocking seemed to sicken the bairn and she vomited. This seemed to help and Teenie was better for a time, and Megan rocked and rocked in an effort to get her to sleep.

Meanwhile Jancey lay in the box-bed and coughed and tossed in a restless stupor.

The other bairns had wearied and gone upstairs to bed. Megan prigged with Jonas to stay with her by the peat fire but he said he couldn't sleep on a chair. She kept vigil alone and even the willow-pattern plates took on a sinister expression as she looked at them on the wall racks. They seemed to stare back at her as if she was a stranger among them. Her eyes wandered round the old kitchen to the passage door, where every moment she expected an apparition to emerge from the gloom. She saw visions in the peat flames in the white-washed hearth. The ivy leaves tapped at the window panes with soft ghostly fingers. She closed her eyes and almost fell asleep, till the scratch of a mouse resurrected her fears. Her ankles ached on the cradle rocker and Teenie began to cry again. Would Sarah never come?

Jancey coughed and coughed till Megan thought she was going to die. The long brass pendulum on the wag-at-the-wa' clock swung the hours away. The seconds were measured out into minutes with every beat of its iron heart. The minutes were circled into hours by the fretted fingers on its flower decked face. Two rocks of the cradle to the long deliberate swing of the pendulum, hour after hour, until it seemed an eternity. And Teenie still puckered her face in agonised spasms of pain.

Megan's eyes rested on the brass knob of the closet door. It reflected the firelight like a beacon. She could almost imagine that it was turning and that the door would open. But the peat flames played a devil's dance on the brass berry-pans under the dresser, they shone like full moons and laughed at her fears.

Would Sarah never come?

But Gleg and Sarah were in nae mood for gaun hame. They stayed with the Blossoms folks into the sma' 'oors o' the mornin'. After all it wasn't often that they got a night out, and with Megan in charge at home there didn't seem to be much to worry about. The shilt had been stabled with an oxterful of hay and a leepy-ful of bruised corn; the nicht was fine and the peat fire was warm, so there was nae thocht for the lang road hame.

Sarah even forgot for a time aboot Jancey and Teenie that were ailin' at Kelpieside, though she had tel't her mither aboot the bairns. But they hadna been sae bad these last few days and the doctor was lookin' in bye noo and than. Sarah's mither gave her a tot of brandy to warm her up after her journey in the gig. It helped her to forget things that mattered for a time and she stopped worryin' aboot her bairns.

Gleg too had a fair swig o' whisky frae auld Basil. It lightened his mind and loosened his tongue as he shared his troubles with his father-in-law. And there was this body tae rake up and yon crater tae ring doon, craps and beasts and prices tae be taen thru' haun, gweed kens whaur the time gaed till. The tea was good (even withoot melk for Sarah) and Gleg's pipe tasted real grand after the whisky. Old Basil Blossom, Sarah's father smoked a pipe as well, a clay pipe with a fich on't and they could hardly see each ither for reek.

"Weel weel, gweed kens, but we'll hae tae be goin'," Gleg said at last, as he knocked out his pipe in the peat ash. Basil took the lantern and went out with him to yoke the shilt into the gig. Sarah put on her nap coat with the ivory buttons and seated herself on the gig, high above the wheels. Gleg tucked her in with the rugs and she nestled her hands in her muff. He lighted the candle lanterns and you could see the shilt's breath in the flutter of light. "Gweed nicht then," said Gleg, and climbed into the seat with Sarah. Next moment they were off, driving into the night.

"I hope Jancey and Teenie are a' richt at hame," said Sarah;" and if we see yon jacket on the road hame we'll stop and pick it up."

The moorhens were silent on the heather and as Gleg approached Lachbeg Woods Sarah watched for the jacket. Sarah had marked the spot well and though it was dark she would get a glimpse of it in the light from the gig lanterns. Gleg slowed the shilt to a trot and the clip-clop of his hoofs rang sharp and clear in the dark silent woods.

But the jacket was gone and in its place a ball of light flooded the roadway, sudden, silent, mysterious. Sarah was frightened. She clutched tightly at Gleg's arm and nearly tore the reins out of his hands. "Oh Daw," she cried, "My bairns!"

Two angels appeared, one on each side of the road, gliding along beside the gig, the light shining on their wings. Sarah was terrified and her scream woke the night. The shilt neighed loudly and rose in the air and toppled Gleg and Sarah out of the gig. Gleg kept hold of the reins but even as they fell Sarah saw the light rise up to heaven with two angels in the midst of it, shining through their wings; up and up until she must have fainted, because the next thing she remembered Daw was holding her in his arms and shaking her back to consciousness.

"Fireballs come doon usually," Gleg said to folk years later about this night, "but this ane gaed up, rose frae the road like a sunrise."

"And twa angels appeared," said Sarah, her face all goose-pimples when she spoke of it. "I saw them fine; they ran along beside the gig, one on each side o' the road, then they rose up in the air, slowly, the licht shinin' in their wings, until they disappeared."

"She fainted," Daw said. "I couldna say I saw ony angels but the shilt saw something, 'cause he reared up and coupit us oot o' the gig."

"And when it was a' by we were left in darkness," Sarah chimed in," the gig was coupit and the lichts went oot and we were baith in the ditch. But we were none the worse. Daw soon had the shilt in hand again and we managed hame in the dark.

"But I was that shaken I could hardly stand on my feet, and I kent fine it was my bairns; a warnin' frae Heaven that my Jancey and Teenie wad soon be taen awa'. I could hardly wait or we got hame.

"Ah weel," Sarah continued, "Teenie died in the mornin', my poor wee Teenie, and never opened her een for me at the last. The doctor said Jancey had consumption; tuberculosis he called it, and she didna last lang after Teenie. Aye, poor Jancey, she had a hoast like an auld roosty pump, and never stoppit yarkin' frae daylicht tae dark. She lived only twa days efter Teenie died. I took her on my knee tae gie her a doze o' Ipecacuanha wine and the poor thing never got it doon. She choked in my airms and turned blue in the face. I thumpit 'er back tae get her breath back but it was nae use. Next meenit she was deid. We had a double funeral. Poor Jancey and Teenie; Janet and Christian was their real names but the ither bairns could never get their tongues roon't.

"My poor Jancey and Teenie," Sarah sobbed, "my twa wee angels. They were too good for this world. Efter yon nicht in Lachbeg Wuds I can believe they are in Heaven. Yon twa angels were waitin' tae tak' them hame!"

I WADNA BE A LOON AGAIN

Every mornin' at five sharp Knowie came up the stone stair at
the back and rapped with his knuckles on my chaumer door.
"Are ye waukened lad?" he cries, waiting for an answer. I
could have seen him in Purgatory but I says "Aye aye!" and
slid out of bed, cold as a seal on an iceberg. I had to light the
old paraffin lamp where it hung on the wall, shell-backed and
leaking, to let me see to put my clothes on, although the rest of
the steading was lit by electricity, generated on the premises.

Down in the byre Knowie fed the kye with draff and bruised
corn while I mucked them out with barrow and shovel. He
scrubbed their hind-quarters with a long-handled broom,
dipping it in a pail of cold water as he went along. The cows
swished their lithe bushy tails in my face, sprinkling my neck
and bare arms with cold icy drops, which soon shook me out of
my sleep.

Twenty-four cows stood in a single row, heads to the wall,
tails on the greep, licking their food out of rough-faced cement
troughs. Drinking bowls were not then in existence so there was
a water cistern at the far end of the byre, fodder barn and
turnip shed at the other.

At five-thirty Knowie's wife and two daughters came in for
the milking. They brought their cans and pails from the dairy
and took down their stools from a shelf. They sat down, each
one to a cow, and very soon they had brimming pails between
their knees, spurting the hot milk into the rising froth in
rythmic, steady jets, plop-plop, plop-plop. . .

All this time young Knowie had been feeding the horses and mucking out the stable, his own pair and my odd horse, old Bud, a proper bitch with teeth and hoof; dark brown with white rings in her eyes, and her ears mostly flat back on her mane: "Ringle eyen an' her lugs in the howe o' her neck," as they say, and supposed to be a sure sign of equestrian temperament.

Aleck was foreman on the place, but folks behind his back just called him young Knowie, sometimes with a bit of a sneer, 'cause the folk at the Knowehead were a bit stuck-up they said, and young Knowie was the glowerin' image o' his auld man, but less high-minded.

We went into breakfast, Aleck going first, him bein' foreman at the Knowehead, and his auld man liked him to have his thumb on the sneck o' the kitchen door at the hour appointed. Knowie came in after us to wash and shave for the milk round. While we slubbered away at our brose and cream he laid off about the work that had to be done in the forenoon, a screed as lang as a kirk sermon, and it made denner time seem an affa distance awa'. When his back was turned Aleck gave me a wink. "We'll juist dee what we've time for!" says he, sort of under his breath, for he was still a bit feared at his old man, him bein' only a haflin.

But I was heartened by the label on the syrup tin, which read: "Out of the strong came forth sweetness!" And there was a swarm of bees bizzin round the carcase of a lion that the mighty Samson had slain with his bare hands.

After breakfast we laced our boots by the kitchen range and stytered out in the darkness to the stable. We were supposed to kaim the horse but we knew that old Knowie was at his porridge so we lay down among the straw in the spare stall. I had a bit blow at my pipe and Aleck lit a fag, never saying a word to spoil it, but each one enjoying his own thoughts. Then we fell asleep. The next thing we hears is the purr of the lorry and the rattle of milk cans, which was Knowie loading up for the town.

We sprang to our feet and grabbed a brush and comb, nipped up beside a mare and banged away at the travis posts. The noise was enough to frighten the rottans off the rafters and Knowie fair thocht he had a pair of gallant grooms. Sometimes he took a bit keek into the stable with a last minute order but never once did he catch us on the straw. Then he got into the lorry cab and slammed the door. The headlights swung round and searched out the trees in the avenue, whining down to the main road.

The women had finished the milking and gone to the farmhouse (while we were asleep) for there was no cooling system to scutter with in those days, and the milk went into the cans warm from the cow's udders.

Aleck harnessed his pair, "Jip" and "Tib," for the plough, while I went back to the byre to finish the work of the morning. I fed the cows with neeps and hay, mucked out the byre again and bedded them down with fresh clean straw. I gave each cow a drink in a bucket from the cistern at the end of the byre; honest, I did, every cow, for I've heard of the lad who poked his finger in the cow's eye when she wanted a drink, and a pailful went a long way — the thing is that you put the water in the cow, not in the can. Then I splashed and scrubbed the greep with Knowie's long-handled broom

When rosy dawn began to tint the east I opened the big sliding door on the dung court and turned the twenty odd heifers out to winter pasture. I then went to the stable to harness old Bud for the cart, driving home turnips till dinner time.

I had to stand on my toes to force the hard leather collar over Bud's stubborn head, upside-down to get it over her bulging eyebrows, then swivel it round on the narrowest part of her neck. You had to have an extra spoonful of meal in your brose for this job, and I've known some lads having to stand on a box, or the "corn leepy", aye, even grown men, to manage it. Another tussle was getting your saddle off the saddle-tree high up on the wall, when you carried it on your head to your mare's back, then fastened the belt under her belly; and even at this you had to be careful, or Bud would bite or kick your backside, which ever way you bent down. But as I was of fair average height I managed these jobs on my feet, so that nobody could look down their nose at me, or take me to the "chaff hoose," where you shook hands with the devil, and then you could do almost anything with a horse, or so they said.

But the first morning I tried to collar Bud she backed out of the stall and bolted from the stable. She meant to take me all round the parish at her heels, but I got her on to the sharn midden, where she floundered to the belly, and I had no more ado than halter her. She meant to sit on the warm muck till dinner time, but I stuck a whin bush under her tail and she soon changed her mind about that.

After that I always closed the stable door before I tackled Bud. I tried another way: I put the saddle on first, which meant I didn't have to loosen her halter chain, but she leaped into the forestall, and the saddle went slithering over her back and fell on the cobble-stones among the dung. One of her fore feet got stuck in the manger and she was standing on three legs. I took advantage of the situation to get the saddle on, but I couldn't manage the collar in this position. I removed the halter and eased Bud's foot out of the forestall, but she sprang backwards out of the stall and ran back and forth in the stable, from one end to the other, while I tried to corner her to get the collar on. This time she nearly had me in tears. She finished up in the wrong stall, and I had to carry the harness piece by piece — collar, haimes, britchen, bridle and reins from the other end of the building. Fortunately the saddle remained on her back, and prance as she would she couldn't get rid of it.

Bud had sharp teeth and quick hoofs that went with her bad temper. She knew that I was only a loon and she wouldn't have tried it on with a grown man, not with those "strappin' cheils" who knew the horseman's word, and all that stite.

Knowehead bein' a "three-horse place", Bud had never worked with another beast as a "pair" but always as the odd horse, and always handled by a loon, so that I was only another in a long succession of loons whom she had taken the size of, for she was a wily beast was our Bud.

When there was ice on the roads I had to take the mare's fetlocks between my knees from behind, as the blacksmiths did, and hammer spikes into the holes in her iron shoes. At nightfall I had to chisel them out again, or have her stand all night on her stilettoes, which was what she deserved. That frosty mornin' I went to the toon without spikes or "sharps", as they were sometimes called, Bud went slithering down the Broadgate like a new born calf on a wet greep.

Knowie supplied some of the town carters with quantities of hay and straw, and I had to take this through their narrow pends and low arches, terrified that Bud got stuck with a load in a pend, and besides this I had to take the occasional load of corn to the granary, ten sacks to the load.

When mother fee-ed me off as a loon she never knew what she was letting me in for with our Bud at the Knowehead.

And there was that great muckle stone at the cartshed door: It was so important I should have carried it around on my watchchain, yet it was all I could do to heave it into the cart. Knowie had told me about the stone at the cartshed door the night he fee-ed me in the parlour, the only time I had ever been ben the hoose; and I was never likely to see the parlour again, unless I married one of Knowie's dothers, and there was small chance of that, because that verra nicht he made me promise that I wouldn't try to sleep with the lassies. He said it in a jocular sort of way, if you could say that Knowie was capable of a joke.

After this, and when he made me swear that I didn't wet the bed, and that I didn't carry lice, he told me what I had to do with the stone at the cartshed door, as you shall see.

Bud had a habit of bolting out of the cart at lowsing time, before the shafts were clear of her back, so I had to put the stone in the back of the cart before I loosened the chains on the haimes and britchen. I kept hold of the reins and held Bud by the bridle while I tipped up the shafts with my free hand, and then the stone tilted the balance and lifted the shafts clear of the mare's back. She pranced about and chewed on the iron bit impatient to have it over, but no harm was done.

This was something that Bud was really afraid of. She had probably been held in a cart and got a fright as a young mare and never got over it. But I can hardly imagine our Bud on the psychiatric couch and the vet probing her sub-conscious mind.

Then, one evening, I forgot to put the stone in the cart, and when I tilted the shafts they came down again on Bud's back. She lurched forward and sprang in the air, wrenching herself free of the cart and its trappings. I couldn't hold her and everything snapped; a britchen sling caught on a shaft hasp and swivelled the saddle under her belly — one more leap and Bud was free, and the cart shafts clattered on the ground.

Bud made a run for the stable door, where she stood in a tremble, the saddle still upside-down under her belly, and a trail of broken harness behind her. Knowie came running from the byre, where he had heard the mischanter. "Ye're gettin' a bittie over-confident wi' that beast!" says he, looking at the bits of harness trailing behind her, and no doubt thinking of the saddler's account for mending it. "Aye man, a bittie careless. Ye had forgotten on the steen ah doot! Better see and nae lat it happen again!"

I suppose his attitude would have been the same though I had been crippled for life, for he never so much as asked if I had been hurt. That mare could have killed me, a fifteen-year-old loon, for it was a man-sized job to handle her. The insurance lads wouldn't stand for it nowadays. Twice she had nearly split my knee-cap with an iron heel, doubling me up with pain and sickness, and she bit my shoulder when I went up with her corn feed. She bit the hand that fed her, our Bud, and mother saw the marks of her teeth on my bare skin when I changed my sark at the weekend.

Once a week I went to the railway station for a load of draff as cow feed. It wasn't bad really on a fine morning, seated on the fore shelvin' of the cart, looking down on Bud's broad mobile back as she swung down the brae, her white fetlocks swinging under the cart, while she shook her head and snorted the hay-seed out of her nostrils.

At the station I had to queue with about thirty other carts until my turn came for loading up with my shovel from a waggon. It was an occasion of great bustle and rivalry, each man trying to get his horse backed to a waggon when another drew away. But first you had to pass over the weighbridge to let the station clerk get the tare of your cart. Some of the men had two carts, belonging to the larger farms, and sometimes they had to leave a horse standing by while they loaded the other. Bein' the loon I had to nip in somewhere at the risk of getting my lug clapped, or I wouldn't be home or dinner time.

Some of the lads had high piked haimes and harness beetle black, chains and buckles shining, while others had harness as grey as the road and carts that hadn't seen paint or a wash for mony a year and day.

Bud didn't like the trains, and if the engine-drivers were banging the trucks about I had to keep the reins within reach while I was in the waggon. Not that I could have held Bud had she bolted, but it was a pretence that I was doing my best in the circumstances. And if a passenger train came thundering in you certainly had to hang on to the reins; what with the great hiss of white steam, the banging of carriage doors, the waving of flags and the hub-bub of voices Bud's head was in a whirl. The engine on the down train always stopped near the siding and before leaving again the driver blew the whistle for devilment, a piercing shriek that sent the horses neighing and prancing at the waggons. He got a lot of fist waving from the fairm lads but he didn't care a damn, for he was soon out of their reach in belching steam.

I filled and trampled my cart with steaming draff, hot from the distillery vats, and for one day in the week my feet were warm enough.

I led Bud over the weighbridge and propped up the shafts with the resting-pole to get a better reading, just enough to slacken the backchain in the saddlecrup (for I knew Bud's tricks) while the clerk adjusted a sliding marker on a metrical bar, figured in brass and swinging with the load on the platform, and then he checked my gross weight in his notebook.

Once clear of the station (making sure there wasn't a train going under the bridge when I crossed it) I got on top of the cart and sat on a folded sack. Home at the Knowehead I backed Bud into the turnip shed and shovelled the draff into the feed box, where it was mixed with bruised corn, and then it was time to take Bud from the cart and get ready for dinner.

We were well enough fed at the Knowehead, a fork and knife almost every day, eating meat like the gentry, but the long hours of hard work between the meals made me frightfully hungry. By now I could have nibbled at the draff or a slice of swede turnip in the by going.

It seems strange to me now, forty odd years later, that not a railway waggon remains at that once busy station, now overgrown with weeds and grass and the rails torn up from the siding. All the stir and excitement forgotten, and not a horse left in the district. If I was a loon now, and hadn't experienced it, I would never believe that such things had happened. It makes me feel very old to think that I have lived in an age now gone forever and almost forgotten. The pattern of farm life has changed so completely that I can scarcely believe I was once a loon and saw these things which now are only a memory.

There is a sweet sadness in the thought that I shall never be a loon again, and at the same time a gladness that I shall never again be subjected to the slavery of those far-off days. I am glad that times have changed and that life is easier now for a loon on the land. Even with the prospect of my whole life before me, as it was in those days, I wouldn't exchange my later years for renewed youth, not if going through all that drudgery again was the price I had to pay for it.